THE
Unexpected Death
OF
Father Wilfred

Inspector Wickfield Investigates

Julius Falconer

PNEUMA SPRINGS PUBLISHING UK

First Published in 2009 by:
Pneuma Springs Publishing

The Unexpected Death of Father Wilfred
Copyright © 2009 Julius Falconer
ISBN: 978-1-905809-71-4

Pneuma Springs Publishing
A Subsidiary of Pneuma Springs Ltd.
7 Groveherst Road, Dartford Kent, DA1 5JD.
E: admin@pneumasprings.co.uk
W: www.pneumasprings.co.uk

A catalogue record for this book is available from the British Library.

MA

AN
FGR

To the Clergy
of the Archdiocese of Birmingham

in appreciation

One

*T*he two priests sat opposite each other, at either end of the breakfast table. Fr Wilfred was in his late sixties, a priest of many years' experience, with fingers stained by nicotine, white hair and a slightly stiff manner. He sat stooped in his chair, peering through his heavy spectacles, one of the old school used to the respect of the laity and the immutability of his religion. What did the Second Vatican Council mean to him? It was much ado about nothing. Since nothing can change, as popes and councils had iterated for centuries, why spend three years and a lot of money discussing it? His companion was a young priest in his mid-twenties, with clean, dark features, slender hands and a serious manner. Perhaps his superiors, which is to say principally the archbishop, guided by the comments of the seminary rector and the rural dean, regarded him as a firebrand who would benefit from the steady, case-hardened guidance of his parish priest. His zeal and theological exuberance would be tamed and properly channelled if he spent a year or two with Fr Wilfred; perhaps not so much tamed as crushed out of existence, which would be even better. (This comment is not intended as a criticism of the authorities' good faith.)

Fr Wilfred was engaged in his daily perusal of *The Times*, which he read with apostolic commitment as a religious duty. The priest had a duty to be unworldly, but his parishioners were of the earth, earthy (as St Paul has it), and the priest could not minister with effectiveness if he was totally unaware of the laity's problems and circumstances. With the paper folded several times and propped up against the tea-pot, Fr Wilfred munched his toast and slurped his tea, punctuating his modest meal with comments or exclamations on the themes of his reading: 'disgraceful', 'well, I never', 'what's the world coming to?'. Fr Gabriel, denied the paper until later in the day, sat reading a book – Leo Trese's *Tenders of the Flock*: spiritual but not too heavy for so early in the day – occasionally dabbing spots of tomato sauce from the pages as he consumed the bacon, egg and baked beans which he had cooked for the two of them. The room in which they took their meals was one of the two front rooms of the presbytery, the other being the sitting-room. The dining-room and sitting-room gave out on to the Worcester Road in the centre of the small town. Neither of the priests minded the noise of the traffic very much, as their central position was valued.

When the meal was concluded to the satisfaction of both parties, Fr Wilfred asked his junior what plans he had for the morning.

'My usual study hour, Father,' the younger man said, 'and then I've got the Mass at the school. On my way back, I thought I'd drop in to see old Mrs Buller: I don't think she'll last much longer, and although she's had all we can give her by way of spiritual nourishment, I think she might appreciate a quick visit.'

'Good, good,' Fr Wilfred said, 'and don't forget to tell her she can give us a ring any time – or more likely get her daughter to ring us any time. We mustn't let the dying slip away unnoticed, must we?' Here he looked hard at Fr Gabriel, as if the latter had expressed complete disregard for the dying. It was all part of Fr Wilfred's plan to inculcate the essentials of parish ministry in his young curate whom he suspected of high-flown ideas that would sap the Church's heart's-blood. Prayer, the administration of the sacraments, Holy Mass: what need was there for more? Fr Gabriel sighed inwardly at the inevitability of his superior's comments but was too sensible to give utterance to his thoughts.

In 1968, the year in which the events of this case took place, the Roman Catholic parish of The Sacred Heart and St Catherine of Alexandria, on the Worcester Road, Droitwich, affectionately known as the Pippet Works, after the artist who designed the mosaics in the 1920s and 30s, numbered some 620 permanent Catholic souls, including the Catholic pupils at the two schools, as well as the shifting populations of two hospitals and a nursing home. It was considered a comfortable parish in the archdiocese of Birmingham, a sort of reward for older priests who had demonstrated the virtues of staying-power, conformity and pastoral efficiency. Curates were parachuted in according to their needs – it was taken for granted that all newly ordained priests required further practical training which the seminary years, spent in purdah at Oscott College in Sutton Coldfield, were ill-equipped to provide. A spell at the Pippet Works, as at other similar parishes in the archdiocese, was designed to curb excesses of zeal or innovation and to instil proper observance of sacerdotal conventions. This work had become even more urgent in the wake of Vat II ('VatTwo', as it was almost universally known in Roman Catholic clerical circles), which, according to many, had unleashed diabolical and dangerous forces into Mother Church. Only firm handling would enable the Church to ride out the storm.

Pope John XXIII, patriarch of Venice, a rotund figure in his late seventies, was elected pope in 1958 as a stopgap to keep the papal seat warm until somebody more suitable could be found. His pontifical *gesta* could be considered contradictory. On the one hand he issued the Apostolic Constitution *Veterum Sapientia* ('VetSap' to many of its clerical readers) which urged the recovery of Latin as the universal language of the Church and which many regarded as a retrograde and in any case Canutian step, and on the other he announced the convening of the Church's twentieth general council, at which the world's bishops would assemble to discuss matters of importance and urgency – although there was much dispute as to what should be considered important and urgent. For three years, off and on, bishops, up to 3000 of them at any one time, came and went, assembled in small groups and in plenary sessions, discussed and argued and debated, and eventually they published sixteen documents, with such grand and resonant titles as *Apostolicam Actuositatem* and *Unitatis Redintegratio*, ranging in length from a little over 1000 words to more than 16,000 words. The world yawned and carried on with its business, but for Roman Catholics the globe was tottering on its foundations – or so some, including Fr Wilfred, thought.

The five seminaries of England and Wales could not ignore the council, much as some members of staff might have wished. The various lecturers felt obliged, partly by the bishops themselves and partly by the atmosphere amongst the laity, to feed into their teaching at least some of the insights and sayings of the council fathers, but they did so with various degrees of enthusiasm. No one was exempt from at least appearing to pay respects to the council: the dogmaticians, the moralists, the liturgists, the Church historians, the ecumenists, the pastoralists, the biblicists, all had to read the council documents and take on board whatever it was they were deemed to be purveying. In most cases the innovations were intangible and imponderable, with plenty of scope for variety of opinion and interpretation and fervour, so that some lecturers skimmed over the documents with the briefest nod in their direction, while others took the trouble to sift through them carefully and extract what they regarded as interesting, even dramatic, novelties. The poor students were to some extent caught in a pincer movement, or perhaps tug-o'-war would be a better analogy, pulled towards ever more entrenched tradition fighting for its existence on the one hand, and towards unfettered novelty on the other. Fr Gabriel was the result of this unseemly tussle, to which there did not seem to be an easy solution. Students left the seminaries buoyed up by a sense of change and fresh air and new ideas, and yet unsteady when the props of traditional piety and spirituality were being eroded. Some seminary lecturers might have been guilty of a lack of caution; some might have been guilty of resistance to change. The result was, so Fr Wilfred thought, a mess, and for his part he was determined that none of what he had learned as a seminarian and practised assiduously as a priest for over forty years should be lost, either in his own ministry or in that of the young priest entrusted to his charge.

It was not that Fr Wilfred deliberately flouted the bishops' combined will or took positive steps to reverse conciliar suggestions. It was simply that his way of thinking and his ideas of what was proper in ritual and worship were conservative, and he was afraid, irrationally if the truth be told, of letting go of what worked in favour of untried methods, even at the behest of the world's bishops. There is nothing new in this: the tension between tradition and change is age-old, but it was an attitude not designed to set Fr Gabriel's anxieties at rest.

They had discussed the council at supper, on more than one occasion.

'All this opening up to so-called Christians who follow that heretic Luther can only unsettle the simple faithful,' Fr Wilfred would intone. 'The pope is head of Christ's Church, and anyone not in communion with the pope is doomed. It's as simple as that. The council can't change the facts, so what's all the fuss about?'

'Don't you think, Father, that friendship and communion amongst those who profess to follow Christ are better than argument and hatred?'

'Protestants are wrong, and the way forward is not to ignore that and pretend it's not true but to encourage them to embrace the truth, and that means becoming Catholics.'

'Yes, Father,' said Fr Gabriel, 'but the council admits that all those baptised, into whatever Christian denomination, have the right to be called our brothers and sisters in the Lord.'

'Does it?' was Fr Wilfred's invariable retort. 'It just shows what a lot of nonsense the bishops can talk when they put their minds to it.'

Or else Fr Wilfred would say something like, 'I see the pope's going to have talks with some Jewish leader who's on a visit to Rome. Much good that will do!' To which Fr Gabriel would reply,

'Yes, but Father, the council teaches that the Catholic Church rejects nothing which is true and holy in non-Christian religions. It even says they deserve our esteem.'

'Esteem!' Fr Wilfred would harrumph. 'Why should we esteem error, I'd like to know. No, no, give me the *Syllabus of Errors* any day.'

In this vein, life continued uneasily, with Fr Wilfred insisting on the standards which he found acceptable, and Fr Gabriel trying desperately to introduce some measure of change and, as he saw it, enlightenment, into parish practice, and, in his own thoughts, reconciling the two. Now one factor worked in the latter's favour. As a youthful, energetic and zealous priest, Fr Gabriel made it his business to carry out his pastoral visiting. During the day, he hunted up the house-bound or shared with Fr Wilfred the pastoral care of those in hospital or at school. In the evenings, he toured the parish on his bicycle, visiting two or three families each evening, sitting with them for an hour or so, getting to know them, asking for their opinions, urging them to more assiduous parish practice or thanking them for their help. Fr Wilfred, on the other hand, had lost a little of his fire. His view was that the parish, by which he meant church, presbytery and parish-hall – the buildings - was the centre of

Catholic life in Droitwich, and his parishioners should make it their business to visit as often as possible. Instead of *his* visiting *them*, as he had done as a young priest, *they* should visit *him*. In most cases he was available or would happily make himself available. Now parishioners with young families and those who were themselves elderly felt that a weekly visit on a Sunday and a monthly trip to confession were sufficient attention to the routine maintenance of their souls, and few found the time, energy or goodwill to look Fr Wilfred up in his presbytery. Fr Gabriel, it therefore transpired, saw more of the parishioners than his superior did, and his youth and openness and well-favoured manner were not long in making their mark.

Two episodes will illustrate perfectly Fr Gabriel's commitment to his vocation through the difficulties associated with living a celibate life in an alluring world. He was sitting reading late one evening in the presbytery when there was a prolonged ring at the front door. He put down his book, imagining an imminent death or perhaps a road accident at which his ministrations were required, opened the front door and saw on the doorstep a woman of about thirty who was clearly distressed. He did not recognise her.

'Father, Father,' she panted, 'please come quickly!'

'Why, what on earth's the matter?'

'My husband will be home from the pub soon, and I know he plans to beat me up, but if you were there, he wouldn't. You must come and talk to him: it's urgent.'

Young Fr Gabriel was not quite sure how to react, and unfortunately Fr Wilfred, who was away visiting family for a few days, was unavailable for advice. He asked a few more questions of the woman and finally agreed to accompany her back to her house. She rushed round to the driver's seat, opened the passenger door for him from inside, and within a few seconds the car had sped off. It seemed to the priest that the fast journey in the rain took him a considerable distance beyond the parish boundaries; in fact he was sure he recognised the outskirts of Bromsgrove, but in the pouring rain it was difficult to be certain. Eventually the car skidded to a halt.

'Quick, Father, we're just in time.'

She let them both into the house and told him to make himself comfortable in the sitting-room while she made tea.

'He will think it's a routine parish visit,' she said, 'and you must tackle him about his drinking.' She disappeared into the kitchen, whence issued the clink of cups and spoons. However, only a few minutes elapsed before she reappeared, but this time as naked as the day she was born. She made to dive at him as he sat on the sofa. Fr Gabriel, naturally fearing for his virtue, leapt to his feet and headed at full speed for the front door. There, the combination of perspiration on his hands and the lock's being on the latch prevented him from making a rapid exit. He fumbled with the door as his hostess pawed him from behind. At long last he succeeded in wrenching himself free and stumbled into the night, where a long and wet walk awaited him. He chalked the episode up to experience.

The other occasion was spread over several weeks, indeed months. A woman called Rosie (not her real name) conceived an attachment for the young priest which exceeded the bounds of Christian respect. She had consulted him in the first instance concerning a relationship which was causing her problems, in that she felt that her inclinations were moving her away from her duties as a Christian. The object of her affections was a married man who was hesitating over a break from his wife in order to marry Rosie, and her conscience troubled her. The result of Fr Gabriel's sympathy and counsel was simply a transfer of Rosie's affections to him, and he found himself the object of an intense obsession which threatened to unseat his priestly equilibrium. Rosie was young and expansive and charming, and it would have taken the misogyny of a St Jerome to deny her attractiveness. The young priest prayed, and prayed more fervently, unwilling to throw himself unclothed into a bed of stinging nettles, as St Benedict is reported to have done, to quench the stirrings of desire. Eventually he had the good sense to consult Fr Wilfred, and he, nothing loath, visited the woman in her home to warn her off. He also forbade her entry into the church and presbytery: she would have to attend Mass elsewhere. There was no other Catholic church in Droitwich, but St Peter's in Bromsgrove would afford her a welcome. Rosie's personal contacts ceased, but her letters began, long epistles expressive of her longing and loneliness and frustration. After some weeks of strangling this unilateral correspondence at birth, by the simple expedient of tearing the letters into shreds almost as soon as they dropped through the presbytery letter-box, Fr Wilfred again went round to remonstrate with Rosie. Realising that the Rhinegold was guarded by a dragon every bit as fearsome as Fafner, Rosie's ardour was finally stifled. Fr Wilfred contemplated with satisfaction the happy results of his labours, whilst Fr Gabriel was filled with compassion for Rosie, thwarted desire at what he might have missed, and relief that his priesthood was intact after the rude assault on its defences. He supposed he was strengthened in his vocation by the trial to which it had been subject, but he regretted the misogynist and narrow view which had turned clerical celibacy into an imposition instead of a choice.

The day of the breakfast with which this chronicle began was a Thursday, and by tradition there were confessions and Benediction in the evening. Not many attended, but at least the clergy could say that the opportunity was there for the more spiritual parishioners who wished to avail themselves of it. Like the rosary and other mechanical devotions, Benediction and confession were slowly slipping out of fashion, particularly with the younger generation but also with the better educated laity in general. The priests took it in turns to officiate, while the other was free to attend, or undertake pastoral tasks, or begin the preparation of his sermon for Sunday. It was Fr Wilfred's turn to officiate, and punctually at six-thirty he was ready in the confessional, becassocked and stole'd for the ministry of the sacrament of penance. A few people were in the church, waiting in the short queue for confession, or telling their beads, or lighting candles in front of the Lady statue. Most of them were elderly, or at least middle-aged. Because it was a day in February, the lights were on in the church, and a little heating. The justly celebrated mosaics gleamed in the half-light, with the majestic robed figure of Christ, with arms outstretched in welcome, which dominated the church from above the apse behind the high altar, picked out with a spot-light. The scene was one of calm recollection before the short service of adoration of the Blessed Sacrament. In the normal way of things, the priest would leave the confessional at five minutes to seven, to don the heavy, elaborate cope while a server lit candles on the altar and prepared the monstrance. On this particular evening, the confessor made no move to leave his perch in the confessional, and yet there was no one having his confession heard or waiting outside the confessional. The small congregation were uncertain how to proceed, until the server, a retired school-teacher called Basil, said he would rouse the priest and alert him to the time. It sometimes happened that the priest lost track of time, or dozed off, or was simply absorbed in prayer (as the more charitably minded parishioners preferred to think).

The confessional was a free-standing, wooden structure, consisting of three segments: the central enclosed seat for the confessor, and open spaces on either side where the penitents knelt. The example at the Sacred Heart was particularly rich in decoration, with coffered panels, guilloche and chevrons, a frieze with mitred lozenge moulding and an architrave. If the priest chose to close the doors to the shriving-pew, he could not be seen from outside, but mostly Frs Wilfred and Gabriel left the doors ajar so that the parishioners could note their presence. At the same time there was a curtain across the doorway which concealed the confessor's upper torso and face. Between the confessor and the penitent was a metal grille, at eye level for someone kneeling. On the priest's side of the grille was a shutter which the priest manipulated to close off one side of the confessional from both sight and sound so that he could turn his attention to the penitent waiting on the other side of the shriving-pew. The wings of the confessional-box projected sufficiently to conceal from someone facing the box from directly in front all of the penitent's body but his or her feet.

Basil tentatively approached the doors of the confessional, from which vantage point he could clearly see Fr Wilfred's becassocked midriff. He coughed, softly at first, and then more loudly. There was no movement from within, and Basil was bold enough to move the curtain aside. There was Fr Wilfred, with his eyes closed, to all appearances deep in contemplation of the Almighty – or perhaps, of course, of the Sacred Heart (which would be very fitting) or of the Virgin Mary. Basil wondered whether he should interrupt a trance so deep; perhaps the confessor, exhausted by his pastoral ministrations at the end of a busy day and ripe with years of devotion to the Lord now, on this spot and minutes before Benediction, to be crowned with a mystical reward, was enjoying a Teresian ecstasy that should be recorded in marble, *à la* (perhaps more properly *alla*) Bernini! A few coughs from behind him warned him that action on his part, not deliberation, was required, and he quickly moved to wake the snoozing priest, shaking him gently by the shoulder. Fr Wilfred tipped forward without a murmur of protest and tumbled out of the confessional at Basil's feet, landing in an ungainly and undignified heap on the tiled floor. The back of his cassock rose to reveal a stockinged leg, the stole spread out into the aisle, and his spectacles tinkled brittlely as they fell off his nose. Fr Wilfred would never hear confessions again.

Two

*T*hose assembled in the church, perhaps a dozen persons all told, were dismayed. They moved as one to stand round the priest, gazing down at his corpse in stupefaction.

'Well,' said one, 'it's no use our standing round like dummies. Let's move the poor man into the sacristy.'

Two or three men scooped him up, a little clumsily, and carried him into the sacristy, but it soon became apparent that the only chair there, a wooden structure with a narrow seat and low arms, was quite unsuitable to contain a corpse, and the decision was quickly taken to move the priest into the presbytery. There Fr Wilfred was laid to rest on the sofa in the living-room, composed with as much dignity as the parishioners could achieve.

'He's quite gone, I'm afraid,' said an elderly woman, 'but we'll have to get a doctor, won't we?'

Since neither Fr Gabriel nor the house-keeper, who did not live in, seemed to be on the premises, one of the parishioners took it on himself to telephone for the doctor, and the little group then stood around aimlessly, engaging in desultory conversation, unwilling to return to the church and so abandon the scene of the little drama. The doctor eventually put in an appearance, a young man whom none of the group knew, and it took him very little time to diagnose that the small patch of dark red on the front of the priest's cassock was caused by a stab wound in the chest. The onlookers were aghast. Mouths dropped open, but nobody spoke, until an incredulous voice said, 'Are you sure, Doctor?'

'Of course I'm sure, you've only to look for yourself!' came the starchy reply.

Of course the police were called. Initial statements were taken. Names and addresses of all those present were recorded. In short, all the normal systems of a murder scene were put in place.

This orderly and time-worn procedure was rudely disturbed, however, by the arrival of a visitor. Fr Wilfred's older, unmarried sister Maud, informed by Fr Gabriel later that evening of her brother's unexpected death, swept into the presbytery on the following morning and took command.

'Stabbed to death? in his own church? whilst engaged in administering the sacrament of confession? This is outrageous. I told the archbishop years ago that Wilfred should never have been sent to this God-forsaken town. Have you reverted to the Dark Ages in Droitwich? I demand a full post mortem, and it will be performed by a friend of the family: no one else will do.'

She kicked up such a fuss with the archdiocesan authorities and the doctor and the undertaker and Fr Gabriel and the parish functionaries, telephoning round with her loud opinions and her peremptory orders, that, not surprisingly, she carried the day. It being considered unsuitable for her to lodge in the presbytery, where Fr Gabriel continued to reside, maintaining parish services to the best of his ability in the face of considerable upheavals, she contrived to secure comfortable accommodation at the half-timbered Raven Hotel in the town, and there she took up her billet while what she termed a 'proper' post mortem was put in place. The chosen pathologist, whose report was available the following evening, took the view that Maud's brother had died of a single stab wound in the right-hand side of the chest, between the fifth and sixth ribs, with a short blade the probable dimensions of which were, along with other technical data, given. There was one other finding which the pathologist mentioned: Fr Wilfred had taken a sedative (Librium) some time in the hour, probably in the half-hour, previous to his death.

Although the police had been involved in the case from the start, and the housekeeper had assured Miss Tarbuck that all was in hand, that did not prevent the lady from sailing into the police station in

Worcester early on the morning of her arrival and demanding instant admittance to the policeman in charge of the case.

'My brother's been murdered,' she announced. 'You're to put on this case the best detective you've got, and I want to see him now, if you please.'

She stood at the desk looking formidable and indomitable.

'Yes, Madam, of course. Just let me check who's been assigned. Perhaps you would have the goodness to take a seat for a few minutes.'

The station superintendent returned a little while later with an apologetic cough.

'Our best detective has already been assigned to the case, Madam, and I am sure you will find him most satisfactory.' He said this with a deliberately oily voice which apparently deceived his visitor, who missed its sardonic undertones.

'And who is this detective?' she asked acidly.

'His name is Inspector Wickfield,' the superintendent said. 'He has the reputation of an experienced if, um, slightly unusual member of the CID. I think he'll suit very well.'

'Do you?' she asked. 'Well, let's see him, then.'

At that, Inspector Wickfield appeared at the foot of the stairs and advanced to meet the fair inquirer. The inspector was tall and craggy, with a large nose and glasses perched on its bridge. His hair and his clothes were equally unruly, but there was an intelligence and a kindliness in his eye which disarmed all but the most aggressive. The lady was tall and bosomy, with flowing clothes and a broad-brimmed hat, a heavy face and a loud voice. Their encounter must have been satisfactory, because ten minutes later, Miss Tarbuck swept out of the station with her head high and a thin smile on her rouged lips.

Wickfield returned to his office and summoned his sergeant, Spooner, who was relatively new to his post. In appearance Spooner was what in the olden days would have been called comely: good clean features, an intelligent eye, a pleasant manner, and always neatly turned out. Wickfield and Spooner were to form a team for seven years all told, the intuition and flair of the one meshing with the methodical and more prosaic approach of the other.

'Well, now, Sergeant,' Wickfield said in what he hoped was a business-like tone. 'I haven't had a chance to see you since last night, but there's another case for us, and I've just met a very forceful lady who thinks that "we'll do"! Let's hope this case is easier than the last one.'

'What have we got, Sir?' Spooner asked.

'What we have got, Sergeant, is a dead priest in Droitwich, and that's about all we know. I have had a, er, chat with this forceful lady, who is the dead man's sister, and she tells me that her brother was surrounded by enemies.'

'Enemies? in Droitwich?'

'Quite so. She tells me that her brother was a staunch and solid supporter of the traditions of the Roman Catholic Church, and that subversive elements in the congregation were intent on undermining his authority and all he stood for.'

'Good heavens! And somebody murdered him for that?'

'Well, let's reserve judgment, shall we? I'm only telling you what Miss Tarbuck told me.'

'Did she name names?'

'No, but she said that we need look no further than her brother's young curate and the clique he had assembled about him. They are apparently determined to savage the Church by abandoning the teachings and practices of centuries in favour of some innovation called Vatican II.'

'Are feelings running so high?'

'According to our Miss Tarbuck, the parish is in a ferment over changes foisted on the innocent laity by maverick bishops, and Fr Wilfred – that's her brother – was at the forefront of efforts to oppose the innovators. He had mentioned to her more than once, it appears, that the Church was slipping into mayhem, and that he was determined that his parish would be a bulwark against the wiles of the devil.'

'Crikey! It's probably nothing to do with that, you know, Sir. Some anti-clerical crank took a swipe at an easy victim, or he was murdered because he'd accosted some matron – could be anything.'

'You're quite right, we mustn't let our judgment be clouded by the opinions of one person, however close to the victim. So let's get started, shall we?'

The two men, Spooner at the wheel, covered the short distance to Droitwich in a quarter of an hour and parked in the church car-park. They were met, by appointment, by the curate, Fr Gabriel, who looked, as well he might, harassed, and by Basil Jennings, the server who had been officiating on the previous evening.

'Gentlemen, we're very glad to see you,' the priest said. 'This has been a great shock to the parish. Unheard of!'

'We shall need to speak to you at some length, Father, as you'll no doubt understand, but for the moment we'd just like to see the scene of the, er, crime.'

'Yes, of course,' Fr Gabriel said. 'Come right in.'

The church, unlit at that hour on a Friday morning, was rather gloomy, particularly so in February, and Fr Gabriel asked Mr Jennings if he would be kind enough to slip into the sacristy (in Roman Catholic parlance: vestry to Anglicans!) to illuminate the body of the kirk. The detectives asked Mr Jennings to take them through Fr Wilfred's last moments.

'Well,' he said, 'we were both in the sacristy. I was cleaning some candlesticks, as I usually do on a Thursday. I helped Fr Wilfred on with his stole, just to the extent of checking that it wasn't twisted at the neck. He then said something about offering God's forgiveness to the faithful and what a joy it was, and then disappeared into the church.'

'Excuse my interrupting,' Wickfield said. 'Did he seem all right to you?'

'Oh, yes, perfectly. He enjoyed the penitential ministry, and he always looked forward to Benediction. He was in an almost jovial mood, I thought.'

'More than usual?'

'No, no, just his usual self. His manner outside church was perhaps a little severe, stiff, if you get my meaning, but he was always cheerful when it came to church services.'

'Yes, please go on.'

'Well, that's about it, really. I didn't see him once he left the sacristy, but I presume he walked straight to the confessional, went inside and sat down. That would be the natural routine.'

'Yes, well, I daresay we can check on that easily enough: someone in the church will have seen him. It was you that found him dead, was it?'

'It was. My, what a shock I got. He just fell out of the confessional, a dead weight – if you'll pardon the phrase.'

Wickfield and Spooner asked to be shown the sacristy and the wardrobe for the vestments. They then retraced the confessor's few steps to the confessional, and there the inspector asked to have the ritual and sequence of confession explained to him. Fr Gabriel obliged.

'Those who intend to go to confession generally sit or kneel in the nearest pews, but they don't have to. There is room for two penitents at a time at the confessional, as you can see,' he went on. 'One kneels at one side and makes his or her confession, while the next one kneels on the opposite side and waits for the priest to open the slide which allows him or her to speak through the grille. When that one's finished, the priest closes the slide and turns to admit the penitent on the other side; and so on. It's an immemorial practice.'

'Can the priest and the penitent see each other?'

'No, because between the slide and the grille there is a thin curtain.'

'And about how many penitents would there have been on Thursday?'

'Oh, five or six, certainly no more. The main time for confession is Saturday morning.'

Wickfield asked whether he might enter the confessional.

'Of course, Inspector. You must do whatever you think necessary.'

The inspector entered the priest's cubicle first, shut the doors, opened them, closed the curtain, reopened it. He then knelt in each wing in turn. He emerged from his inspection looking puzzled.

'I'm not quite sure I see how a penitent, however ingenious, could stab the priest through a grille, a curtain and possibly a sliding door as well. It just doesn't seem possible.'

'But the fact that he died in the confessional means that one of the penitents *must* have done it!' Spooner said. 'All we need do, Sir, is to identify the half-dozen or so penitents yesterday evening, and one of them is our man – or woman, of course.'

'You may be right,' Wickfield said doubtfully, 'and our first job is therefore to find out who those people were. That can't be very difficult, surely?' He turned to Jennings with an eyebrow raised.

'Don't look at me, Inspector! I was in the sacristy most of the time, but your colleagues took the names and addresses of everyone in the presbytery last night, and those who spent the time before Benediction in the church can rapidly draw up a list of those who went to confession.'

'You're right, of course: I should have thought of that myself. Now, Fr Gabriel, is there anywhere you and I can talk?'

'Come into the presbytery, Gentlemen. We'll sit down over a pot of tea.'

The young priest led the way through the sacristy, which communicated directly with the presbytery, and into the sitting-room. He excused himself, in the housekeeper's absence, in order to rustle up some refreshment. (The housekeeper, he explained, would put in an appearance shortly to prepare their – of course, he now meant his – lunch.)

The policemen looked round the room with interest. The surprise was that it resembled any other sitting-room in the land! Quite why they thought it might be otherwise, eluded them. How did confirmed bachelors arrange their living-quarters? Did the housekeeper interfere? Did the priests' mothers and sisters have any say? In a few minutes, the priest reappeared with a tray in his hands, and their preliminary conversation began.

'Fr Gabriel, we regret this disturbance to your ministry, and we hope, of course, that the matter can be cleared up quickly. We shall establish in no time who was at confession, and presumably the last one into the confessional is the culprit, but I'd be interested to find out from you at this stage *why* you think someone should wish to murder an elderly priest, and in circumstances which must make their guilt pretty obvious.'

'That's as much a mystery to me, Inspector, as it is to you,' the priest replied. This smart young man, dressed in clerical black – trousers, shirt and jumper, with a crisp flash of white at the throat – was an engaging if solemn youth, with a hint of Mediterranean swarthiness. There must be some damsels somewhere bitterly disappointed at his decision to enter the Roman Catholic priesthood!

'Let me put you an obvious question,' Wickfield said. 'Had there been any death-threats? Any particular antagonisms? Any trouble? Or does this killing come out of the blue?'

'Is that one question or four, Inspector?' the priest managed with a small smile. 'No, to the best of my knowledge, there has been nothing of the sort.'

'Would you have known about it if there had been?'

'No, not necessarily,' Fr Gabriel admitted. 'We don't make a habit of reading each other's post, but I can say with certainty that Fr Wilfred mentioned nothing to me.'

'Was he himself yesterday?'

'Yes, completely. We'd had a cup of tea together at about half-past four, then I went out to St John's – that's one of the hospitals, you know – and never saw him again; but at half-past four, certainly, he was exactly as he always was.'

'I can't believe someone would murder him out of the blue, so to speak, without any sort of warning or signs of trouble. Let me try to jog your memory. Was there anything in his personal life that you know of that might have given him cause for anxiety?'

'By "personal life" do you mean women, Inspector?'

'No, not necessarily, but presumably priests have family and friends outside their professional duties.'

'That wouldn't really matter, Inspector, would it, if one of the parishioners is responsible, as looks to be the case?'

'No,' Wickfield said slowly. 'Just thinking round the problem, that's all.'

'Well, I didn't really know much about Fr Wilfred's personal life. I've been here only a year and a half, and he never really invited inquiry into how he spent his time off or who he corresponded with. My impression always was that he was more or less absorbed in his ministry.'

'No, I daresay you're quite right and that his personal life has nothing to do with this, but we may have to come back to that later. Let's concentrate for the moment on the parishioners. What motive do you think could lurk behind the killing? Was Fr Wilfred unpopular? Had he made a recent enemy?'

'Well, of course, Inspector, I've been asking myself that question. It is very disturbing to think that a member of our congregation could be so angry and resentful that he commits murder.'

'Or she,' Spooner piped up.

'What?'

'Or she. The killer could be a woman.'

'Oh, yes, I see. Yes, I suppose it could be.'

'So has there been any scene or trouble recently between Fr Wilfred and a parishioner?'

'No, nothing I know of. There are always little tensions, you know, because we can't please everybody all the time, but no, nothing serious.'

'Tensions? What sort of tensions?'

'Inspector, we live in difficult times. You may have heard of Vatican II. It was meant to open the Church up to modern times, but all it has succeeded in doing so far is stir up a whole heap of trouble.'

'Trouble?'

'Let me give you just one example, Inspector. In 1963, public worship in the Catholic Church ceased to be in Latin and was celebrated in English – or in French in France, of course, and so on. At the same time, the altars were turned round so that the priest faced the congregation. Now many of the older parishioners – and clergy – simply couldn't take this. They said the sense of mystery and mystique had dropped out of the Mass; public worship had become a secular tea-party. Meetings were held, a petition was submitted to Fr Wilfred to allow at least one Mass in Latin on a Sunday, some Catholics became disaffected.'

'So what happened?'

'What happened when?'

'When parishioners submitted a petition.'

'Oh, well, I wasn't here then: still studying hard, you know, but nothing happened, apparently. Fr Wilfred said that, by the bishops' diktat, he was forbidden to say Mass in Latin, and that was that: his hands were tied. And there is the question of religious tolerance versus religious liberty.'

'What does that mean?'

'Well, the pre-Vat II Church tolerated other religions: they were all misguided, they were all wrong, but we weren't going to wage war on them for their errors. Vat II seemed to suggest, on the contrary, that other religions were not necessarily contrary to God's will for the world and that people were free to belong to the faith of their choice. People's conscience should be the final arbiter.'

'What's wrong with that?'

'Well, it's obvious, Inspector: it completely undermines the Church's claim to be the sole deposit of truth – whatever truth is. If you can be saved by being a Muslim or a Sikh, why should Catholics try to persuade you to become a Christian?'

'I see. What else?'

'Oh, there were all sorts of things, and it would take me a long time to list the grievances of traditionalist Catholics.'

'Give me one more example. I find this quite fascinating.'

'OK. Vat II said that the Church should be governed not just by the pope but by the pope in conjunction with the bishops.'

'That doesn't seem very controversial.'

'To you it might not, Inspector, but what was called the "collegiality" of Church governance was seen by some as a dangerous innovation. It seemed to weaken the pope's position, and in particular his infallibility, and it seemed to be part of a movement of democratisation of the Church, defying centuries of tradition.'

'And people get worked up about that?'

'Oh, yes, you'd be surprised. Some people take their religion seriously, Inspector.' He said this with an accusatory but quizzical smile in Wickfield's direction, designed, seemingly, to be mischievous rather than discomforting. Wickfield was suitably chastened. As an Anglican, he had none of these problems.

'Well, that'll probably do for the moment, Fr Gabriel,' he said, 'unless the sergeant has any questions?' He turned to Spooner.

'No, Sir, all this theology is a bit beyond me, I'm afraid, and if the murder was committed by one of five or six parishioners who went to confession last Thursday, we can't have much difficulty in nailing the culprit, can we? All this rarified discussion is irrelevant, isn't it, Sir – with respect?'

'Yes, you're probably quite right, Sergeant. Well, Father, thank you for your time. Here's hoping we can wrap the business up in next to no time. All we've discussed this morning is probably, as Sergeant Spooner has intimated, irrelevant. Once we identify the culprit, his or her motive will soon become apparent, I presume. On the other hand, perhaps we should find out *why* Fr Wilfred was killed, and then a culprit will become obvious. Oh, dear, we seem to be floundering already!'

Three

*T*he policemen who had called in at the presbytery on the previous evening had indeed furnished a list of the names of all those who had moved with the body from the church to the priests' living-room and of two people who had been in the church and preferred to stay there. Wickfield and Spooner relied on Fr Gabriel to make discreet contact with some of these parishioners, and later that afternoon they had a list of five worthies who were thought to have confessed their sins to Fr Wilfred in the priest's dying moments. Further inquiry led Wickfield to draw up a list in chronological sequence.

'Well, Sir, surely all we've got to do is to arrest the last one on the list? Simple!'

'Hm, I wish it were, Sergeant, but tell me this: why would someone put themselves so obviously in the limelight? If you were going to kill the priest, why not do it secretly? Why draw attention to yourself quite so obviously?'

'There is that, of course, Sir, but what alternative have we got?'

'Well, for a start, I don't think it can do any harm to interview all five. This will help us build up a picture of all that happened during that last half-hour, and secondly, I've a hunch that not all is at it seems anywhere in this picture.'

'In what way, Sir?'

'Well, this may be a wild and fanciful thought, but what if there was a conspiracy?'

'A conspiracy?'

'It seems just too pat that the last person in the sequence of penitents is the murderer. What if, say, the very first penitent had murdered the priest and then the following penitents had only *pretended* to take the sacrament, talking or at least muttering to a priest whom they knew to be dead?'

'Good heavens, Sir, you have got a devious mind, if you don't mind my saying so.'

'And in that case,' Wickfield continued, ignoring the interruption, 'we have to look for a motive which goes beyond the merely personal and takes in wider parochial concerns, concerns deep enough for murder. Or what if – still thinking aloud, you understand, and this is rather a different idea - the last penitent was set up? The previous penitent actually did the killing – quite how I'm not sure – and the last one in the queue takes the rap? No, all things considered, I don't think we can neglect to interview all the penitents, and then we might have to extend our inquiries to cover all those in the church at the time, and then the wider parish.'

'And I suppose we could eventually find ourselves interviewing the entire archdiocese!'

'There's no need to be funny, Sergeant, but this inquiry is not going to be over in one day, that's for sure.'

To instil solemnity and a sense of serious officialdom into the deliberations, Wickfield chose, with Fr Gabriel's permission, to conduct the interviews in the sacristy, close to the scene of the crime. The parishioners were to be interviewed in order of appearance at the confessional on the fatal evening. They were not yet in a position to make any specific accusations, and all five penitents must be presumed innocent until Wickfield could come up with some coherent case against one of them: motive, opportunity – that was there, all right – and, more dubiously, means. The first to be called forward was a Mrs Veronica Green, a housewife and mother of four. She seemed awed by the surroundings but confident and possibly slightly puzzled as to her role.

'Inspector,' she said, 'I'm not quite sure why I'm here, you know. I went to confession last night, it's true, but Father seemed perfectly all right to me, and I've no idea what happened after I'd come out of the confessional. I went back to my place in church - you know, where I'd left my coat and gloves – and said my prayers, and that's all there was to it.'

'Thank you, Mrs Green, that's exactly what I wished to hear. Now just tell me, will you, exactly what you saw as you waited for confession.

'When do you mean?'

'I mean from the moment Fr Wilfred came out of the sacristy. Where were you at that point?'

'I was kneeling in front of the confessional, at the head of the queue – except that there wasn't really a queue.'

'Could you just explain the convention of queuing?'

'There's no bus-stop sign, if that's what you mean, Inspector: Please queue the other side, that sort of thing. No, there are three pews generally used by those wishing to go to confession, and you shuffle up on your knees as the queue reduces in size. Of course, when there are only a few of you, you know whose turn it is before you, and the queue is then informal, if you get my meaning, or anybody could pop up from anywhere in the church.'

'Thank you. Now please tell us all you saw as Fr Wilfred came out to hear confessions.'

'Oh, I saw nothing, Inspector.'

'Nothing? How was that?'

'I was saying my prayers! I had my head in my hands, and I was just aware out of the corner of my eye of Father entering the confessional. That was the first I knew of him being in the church. I gave him a few seconds to settle, and then went in.'

'When you say "went in", which side did you use?'

'The side towards the altar.'

'Did anything unusual strike you that evening, anything at all? You say Fr Wilfred himself seemed perfectly normal.'

'No, no, I've asked myself that same question many times, but I can't think of a single thing out of place, not one. Yes, Father was his usual self, a little bit gruff and abrupt, but you get used to that.'

The second interviewee was a Mr Christopher Ross, a corpulent, ruddy-faced gentleman on the cusp of seventy, with a game leg and a cauliflower ear. He told the detective team that he was a retired bookmaker.

'Mr Ross,' said Wickfield, 'you will know that we are investigating the death of Fr Wilfred last night. We are interviewing everybody who went to confession, because it was in the confessional that he died, and we hope that one of you will have noticed something that could put us on to the killer.'

Mr Ross clearly thought that this opening remark needed no comment.

'Would you tell us what you can remember about that half-hour?' Wickfield went on.

'Not much. I got to the church at about twenty-five to seven, knelt down to make my preparation, saw that nobody was in the confessional, went straight in and then came out again. I would have stayed on for Benediction, but of course there wasn't any.' Mr Ross's voice had a curious gravely quality, as if he were rolling small stones at the back of his throat.

'Which side of the confessional did you use?'

'Does it matter?'

'Maybe not, but perhaps you could tell us anyway,' the inspector said soothingly.

'Can't rightly remember. Probably the side away from the altar.'

'I see, and did you notice anything unusual?'

'What, about the confessional?'

'Well, yes, but also the church in general, and Fr Wilfred. Did he seem quite normal to you?'

'Everything was perfectly normal, as far as I could tell. I was hoping Fr Gabriel would have been hearing confessions, but it was that old curmudgeon Fr Tarbuck, and yes, he was his usual unsympathetic self.' Wickfield felt unable to comment pertinently on such an assessment, particularly as the poor man was dead.

'Have you any idea why someone would wish to murder Fr Tarbuck?'

'Yes, he was an old stick-in-the-mud, intolerant, old-fashioned, insensitive and stupid. I could cheerfully have murdered him myself if I'd thought of it.'

31

'I see,' Wickfield said, uncertain quite what comment he could suitably make beyond those two neutral words. 'In that case I'm surprised you stayed in the confessional once you'd discovered it wasn't Fr Gabriel.'

There was no answer.

'So why did you stay?' Wickfield repeated.

'Why shouldn't I?' Mr Ross said belligerently. 'I'd come to make my confession, and that's what I did. Nothing wrong with that, I suppose?'

'No, no, nothing wrong at all. Well, thank you, Mr Ross, for your, er, help.'

The third interviewee was a young girl of seventeen or eighteen, a Miss Kylie Bradford, looking pretty in a flowing skirt and a thick woollen jumper, with a mop of well-groomed hair flowing over her shoulders. She clearly found the interview exciting. She was a student.

'May I ask what you're studying, Miss Bradford?' Wickfield asked.

'I'm in my last year at Worcester Sixth-Form College, Officer, doing A-levels.' She smiled sweetly at the two men, crossing her legs again to show a neat piece of shin and a slender ankle.

'What subjects?' Your chronicler confesses freely that this was a ploy on the inspector's part to spin the interview out as long as possible: this history records Wickfield in the raw, so that you may be assured of its veracity.

'Maths, physics and biology.'

'And what do you hope to do with that combination, if I may ask?'

'Medicine,' she said promptly. Realising that he was straying from his script, Wickfield recovered the threads of the evening's work. Nodding at Spooner, the sergeant launched into more appropriate questions.

'Miss Bradford, we understand you went to confession last night, in this church?'

'What, is that a sin now?' she asked archly.

'No, of course not, but you will know by now – who doesn't? – that we are investigating a murder, and we need to question all those who were there at the time.'

'Mm, only having you on, Officer. Take no notice of me.'

'Can you tell the inspector and me exactly what you remember of the evening?'

'Well, I came home from college on the No.12 bus, with my mates – '

'No, Miss Bradford, I mean the time you spent in the church here.'

'Oh, I see. Well, I had something on my mind, so I decided to come to confession and have a quick word with Fr Gabriel – he's really dishy, you know, but perhaps men don't feel about him the way we women do. Anyway, to my disappointment it was that old wet blanket, Fr What's-his-name, so I mumbled a confession and came out. That's all there is to it.'

'Did you notice the other people in the church?'

'No, not really.'

'Which side of the confessional did you use?'

'What on earth has that got to do with it? I went in from the altar side, but I can't see what difference that makes.'

'Did you stay for Benediction?'

'No, it doesn't really appeal to me.'

'So you left the church straightaway?'

'Well, I had to say my penance first.'

'And then you left?'

'Yes, then I left, Officer. You're not doubting my word, are you?' She stared at him with her eye-brows up and a vivacious smile on her lips. Spooner was obviously having difficulty in concentrating on the case, so Wickfield stepped in with a 'Thank you very much, Miss Bradford, you have been most helpful'.

'Don't you want to know why the old priest was murdered?' she asked with something approaching relish.

'If you think you have relevant information, it is your duty to tell us, Young Lady, but we're not here to listen to gossip, you know, and you wouldn't want to be had up for wasting police time, would you, now?'

'Ooh, yes, please, Officer, if that means meeting all the other young policemen at the station!'

'Miss Bradford, do you know anything about the murder, or don't you?'

'Only that he deserved to be murdered, he was such an old fuddy-duddy.'

'So, no, you don't know anything about the murder. Thank you, Miss Bradford, that will be all.' Phew.

The fourth person in the witness-box was a Miss Tabitha Warren, an elderly lady who used a stick to steady her aging legs and had a habit of brushing wisps of grey hair out of her face. To Inspector Wickfield she was the most unlikely murderess he had ever come across, but even though she might not herself be the murderess, she could, even unwittingly, have vital information. Wickfield determined to give his whole attention to the interview, and to that end he invited Spooner to conduct it.

'Miss Warren,' said Spooner in his usual smooth manner, 'we're sorry to be troubling you like this, but you will understand that this is a matter of the greatest importance.'

'That's quite all right, Inspector,' she said.

'Oh, I'm not the inspector, Miss Warren, only a sergeant. This is Inspector Wickfield, Ma'am,' as he waved a hand in Wickfield's direction. 'He's here to see fair play. No, only joking, of course,' he added hastily, as he saw doubt creep across the lady's features. 'Now I want you to tell us, if you would be so kind, exactly what you saw when you were going to confession last evening.'

'Well, Inspector – so sorry: Sergeant – I go to confession every Thursday, you know. It's much quieter than a Saturday morning - no children, for one thing – and I do find Fr Wilfred's advice so helpful. Such a gentle, soothing voice. Oh, dear, such a shock that he's been taken from us.' She paused, with her hand to her nose and a tear in her eye. She quickly resumed. 'Fr Wilfred came out of the sacristy – '

'I'm sorry to interrupt, Miss Warren, but where were you sitting at this point?'

'Opposite the confessional. I saw him come out of the sacristy, make his way across the sanctuary, stop to talk to some gentleman kneeling in the front row and go into the confessional.'

'Just a minute, Miss Warren,' Spooner interjected. 'Could you describe this man in the front pew?'

'No, sorry, Sergeant, I have only the very vaguest impression of him.'

'Thank you, please go on.'

'One or two people went to confession before me, I think, but I was trying out some new prayers of preparation for confession, you see, so I wasn't in any sort of hurry. Someone had given me a prayerbook which contained prayers by St Basil and St John Chrysostom which I hadn't come across before.'

'And which side of the confessional did you use, Miss Warren, when you did go in?'

'I've no idea, Sergeant. Ah, I know what you're thinking. You're thinking that if Fr Wilfred was deaf in one ear, he might not have heard me. But no, Sergeant, he heard me all right, because he made some light-hearted comment about something I said. But thinking back, I must have used the left-hand side, because I approached the box from the top of the church.'

'Did Fr Wilfred strike you as being perfectly normal?'

'Oh, yes,' Miss Warren said. 'As charming and helpful as ever.'

'Do you know what time it was when you went to confession?'

'No, not exactly, but it must have been about ten to, I should think.'

'Did you notice anything suspicious in the church, either before or after you had made your confession, Miss Warren?'

'Suspicious? Certainly not, Sergeant. This is a very respectable church, I'll have you know, and we are all respectable people.'

'Yes, yes, of course,' Spooner put in hastily. 'None the less, you must admit that Fr Wilfred met his death during that half-hour, so not all was as it should have been.'

'Well,' Miss Warren said confidentially, 'whoever it was, I can assure you that it wasn't one of the parishioners. We were infiltrated by a fifth columnist! May I just plant the seeds of an idea in your mind, Sergeant? In *Envious Casca* – you know, that excellent detective novel by Georgette Heyer – the victim is stabbed in the back at the foot of the stairs, but then makes it up to his room – he thinks the pain is his lumbago playing up, you see - locks the door, moves to the bed and does not collapse until that point! What about *that*?'

'Yes, thank you, Ma'am, very interesting, we'll bear it in mind.'

The fifth and last penitent to be interviewed, and necessarily the chief suspect, was a man in his forties, thin to the point of being skinny, prematurely balding, with a stubble on his chin which was not endearing. His name was Thomas Foynes, and he worked as a laboratory assistant at two of the city's schools. He was, Fr Gabriel had told them confidentially, a devout Catholic of the most impressive sort.

'Mr Foynes,' said Wickfield after the appropriate introductions, 'we appreciate your giving up your time to help us with our inquiries.'

'It's a pleasure, Inspector. I'm very anxious to help clear up the murder of poor Fr Wilfred.'

'Good, excellent, that's what we like to hear. Now could you just run over the events of last night in so far as you experienced them?'

'Well, yes, of course, although I'm not sure I can be very helpful. I arrived at the church at about half-past six and sat in my usual pew.'

'Which is where?'

'Towards the front, on the epistle side.'

'"Epistle side"?'

'Yes, on the right of the church as you face the altar – the same side as the confessional, in fact.'

'Um, thank you. Please go on.'

'Fr Wilfred came out of the sacristy, went into the confessional – '

'Excuse me, sorry to interrupt again: did he speak to anyone on his way to the confessional?'

'Yes, to some man in the front row, I think.'

'Could you describe this man?'

'No, not really, he virtually had his back to me. Perhaps a little older than me: mid-forties? Impossible to tell, really. Wearing an overcoat. That's all I can say. Anyway, there were a few people for confession, no real recollection of who they were, and then I decided to go up myself, although I'd really only come to say the rosary and attend Benediction.'

'Did Fr Wilfred seem perfectly normal to you?'

'Well, now you mention it, he didn't. Seemed a bit drowsy to me, sleepy, you know. I just thought he was tired, and I took no notice.'

'Which side of the confessional were you in?'

'That's a funny question, Inspector. In the side nearer the main door: I don't really like to turn my back on the altar, but I can't see what relevance that has.'

'I'm not sure it has. Just thinking round the problem. Now you seem to have been the very last person to speak to Fr Wilfred. You say he seemed to you drowsy or tired. Did he finish the confession?'

'Yes. He pronounced the words of absolution, but rather slowly, while I was making the act of contrition, and then he fell silent. It was all perfectly normal, apart, as I say, from a rather deliberate or sleepy manner.'

'Have you any idea, between ourselves, why someone might have wished to do away with Fr Wilfred?'

'He was not really very popular, Inspector. Not actively disliked, I should say, but most people seem to have preferred the young and earnest Fr Gabriel, who's been in the parish about a year and a half. Fr Wilfred could be a little crusty, and Fr Gabriel was like a breath of fresh air.'

'But you yourself liked Fr Wilfred?'

Mr Foynes paused perceptibly and then said slowly:

'I acknowledged his sincerity. He was well-meaning and honest. He'd been a priest for well over forty years, you know, right through the war, and rationing, and then the permissiveness of the 60s, and he'd stuck to it. I admired him for that, but to say I *liked* him is probably going too far.'

'You must realise, Mr Foynes, that you are the prime suspect in this case, because you were the last person to speak to him. I'm sorry to be so blunt.'

'I know I am, Inspector. What can I say except assure you that I am totally, completely, wholly innocent, in intention and in deed? If I am guilty, perhaps you'd care to tell me how I managed to stab him through the grille? And in any case doesn't it strike you as foolish to put myself in a position where I might so easily be identified?'

'Those are good questions, Sir, and you may be pleased to know that they had already occurred to us. That's probably why we're not arresting you on the spot!' And so the interview ended.

As there seemed no point at that moment in embarking on any further questioning, Wickfield decided to hold a consultation with his junior there and then. He allowed a few minutes so that they could bring their notes into order, and he then asked Spooner what he made of it all.

'Very little, Sir, I'll be honest with you. I have no impression whatever of having just talked with a murderer. We have to presume, I suppose, that the order in which the penitents went to confession on which we've been working is accurate and that the side of the confessional used by those penitents, as told to us, is the true one – not, probably, that that makes a spot of difference. We seem to have a rough time-line: Mrs Green, who went in as soon as Fr Wilfred began the session, say a little after half past six; Mr Ross, who came to the church at twenty-five to seven and went to confession not long afterwards; the skittish Miss Bradford, who went some time between him and Miss Warren; Miss Warren herself, at say ten to seven; and finally Mr Foynes, who was the last one in, leaving at about five to seven, say. Our timings are not accurate to the second, or even to the minute, but I'm not sure it would help us if they were.'

'Yes, a very capable summary so far, Sergeant. Please go on.'

'Well, Sir, I was keenly alert for any hint as to motive. It's got to be a pretty strong motive for murder, hasn't it? Merely disliking someone is not really good enough. I mean, I might dislike the way in which the butcher looks at me when I order the wife's belly pork –'

'Shall we stick to the point, Sergeant?'

'Yes, Sir, sorry, Sir. Now I am getting a feel for certain tensions in the parish, unless I'm deceiving myself, of course, but two other considerations come to mind. One is that generally speaking the young liked Fr Gabriel, and the old liked Fr Wilfred: the parish is to some extent split, if it's split at all, along the lines of age. The second is that what we have heard tonight is probably representative of every Catholic parish in the land, and yet not every parish has its priest murdered in the confessional.'

'So what is your point?'

'Well, I'd like to make two points if I may, Sir.'

'Yes, of course. Please do.'

'One, and here I repeat myself, none of our three female suspects strikes me as the type to stab a holy priest to death in the confessional. A housewife with a family, an elderly spinster clearly doting on her pastor, and a giddy schoolgirl: no, Sir, I just can't see it. Mr Ross might be capable of it, but three seemingly honest people after him in the queue reported Fr Wilfred alive and well. And Mr Foynes? If it's him, how did he do it? And he doesn't seem the murdering sort, if that makes any sort of sense, Sir.'

'And your second point?'

'I think I'd like to know something more about Fr Wilfred, and possibly also about the parish, before we identify a motive or come closer to fingering Mr Foynes.'

'Well, Sergeant, as so often, I concur with you on every point, but I should just like to add a further consideration, at the risk of repeating myself. Fr Wilfred seems to have been perfectly normal that evening except towards the end of the confession session. I just don't see how any of the penitents could physically have got at the priest. They could hardly tape a stiletto to the end of a long stick and poke it through the grille. For one thing, how would they manoeuvre it through the curtain without alerting the priest? and for another, one of the congregation could have seen something if a long stick with a stiletto on the end of it were drawn back ready for the attack. On top of all that, I agree with you that none of our suspects seems to be a likely murderer. Another difficulty we haven't yet mentioned -- and this is where the side of the confessional used by the penitents is important - is that Mr Foynes entered the confessional from the side nearer the main door of the church, and yet the wound in Fr Wilfred's chest was on the right, the side *away* from a penitent on Foynes' side of the box: how could he have reached across the priest and stabbed him from the far side? It doesn't make any sort of sense.'

Four

*T*he following day, therefore – and by now it was the Saturday, two days after the murder, with still no sign of a motive or a means, let alone an arrest – the two men returned to Droitwich presbytery for further information. Fr Gabriel was looking tired. Wickfield asked him how he was coping.

'Oh, all right, I suppose, Inspector, but I admit it's a bit of a strain.'

'What has the archbishop said?'

'Well, a priest is coming out from Oscott – that's the seminary in Birmingham: well, Sutton Coldfield, technically – today to hear confessions and tomorrow to help out with Masses, and he's going to do confessions and Benediction on Thursday. In the long term, the arch will have to put something more permanent in place, but for the moment, it'll do.'

'Good, you're being looked after then – professionally, I mean. By the way, if you hear anything further about the death of Fr Wilfred, you will let us know immediately, won't you?'

'I'll tell you my greatest fear, Inspector: it's to be told in confession who did it and why, and I should be powerless to say anything to anybody.'

'What do you mean?'

'I see you're not a Catholic, Inspector! No shame in that, of course, but let me explain the system. What is said in confession is confidential, totally confidential – on the priest's side, I mean. He can never reveal to any third party what he is told or what he learns in the confessional. The reason is simply that no one would ever go to confession if he thought the priest would then relay information to a third party. There is a story told of St John of Nepomuk, the patron saint of Bohemia, that he was put to death in 1393 for refusing to disclose the secrets of the confessional.'

'How did that come about?'

'Well, it's a long story, Inspector, and it's probably not true anyway, at least not that part of it. Briefly, Wenceslas IV, the king of Bohemia and one of history's cruellest monarchs, suspected his young wife of infidelity and demanded of St John that he reveal the content of the queen's confessions. St John naturally refused, even after threats and torture, and the king had him tied up like a chicken ready for the oven and thrown into the river Moldau, where he drowned.'

'Oh, dear, what a gruesome story. I had no idea the secrecy of the confessional was so greatly valued: it sounds an admirable system.'

'Furthermore, the priest doesn't have to be physically in the confessional to be bound by confidentiality,' Fr Gabriel continued. 'So, for example, a parishioner can speak to a priest at any time – in the presbytery, in the street, in his own home – and caution the priest to secrecy. The priest would be equally bound in those circumstances.'

'Does it work?'

'Oh, most certainly. I've never heard anything to the contrary, and it's a responsibility all the priests I know take extremely seriously, but let me tell you a cautionary tale that we were given as part of our training. I don't know whether it's true or not. A priest was celebrating his silver jubilee, or some such milestone, and after the party with his parishioners, he began to reminisce. "Do you know," he said, "my very first penitent confessed to murder." There were appropriate murmurs of appreciation from his audience. At that, the door opened, and a man came in. "You won't remember me, Father," he said, "but I was your very first penitent." So the lecturer warned us against even hinting at what goes on in confession. I should hate to know who killed Fr Wilfred and yet be unable to do anything about it!'

'What if it happened?'

'All I could do would be to try to persuade the person to go to the proper authorities.'

'I see. Can you avoid hearing confessions for the time being?'

'I doubt it, but I've mentioned the possibility to the arch, and I'm sure he'll do what he can, but I can't avoid hearing confessions for ever and ever, can I?'

'No, I suppose not, but let me tell you why my sergeant and I are here again this morning. We both feel we need a little more information about Fr Wilfred and about how the parish works. As regards Fr Wilfred, I have taken the liberty of contacting the archdiocesan offices at St Chad's to request a file on him. There was no one there, but I left a message and expect – and hope – to hear something on Monday; and I'm asking Sergeant Spooner here to have a word with Miss Tarbuck, if he's brave enough, to see what sort of a picture she gives us of her brother. As regards the parish, I thought a good way in to that latter point was to meet your most active parishioners. What groups meet, and what goes on at them?'

The three men were seated in the sitting-room, the faint sound of the Worcester Road percolating through from the street outside. Catholic papers and other reading matter were scattered about liberally. There were religious artefacts – a statue of Mary, for example – but the pictures were largely secular – a landscape, a seascape, a still life – and the room could possibly have been found in any Catholic household of a certain class in the land. Fr Gabriel put up the fingers of his hand, counting off with the other, while Spooner scribbled away.

'Well, let me see. There's the youth club, the prayer group, the Catholic Women's League, the St Vincent de Paul Society, the choir, Amnesty – although that's not really a *parish* responsibility – marriage guidance, Third World Aid, the Guild of St Stephen, the Guild of St Anne, the Legion of Mary, the Knights of St Gregory, the Knights of St Columba, the Catholic Housing Aid Society, Catenians, and there are probably others I can't bring to mind at the moment.'

'Presumably there's some overlap? Can we eliminate any of the groups, to make our job easier?'

'Well, yes. The Guild of St Stephen is the altar boys: I don't think you need bother with them! and a lot of the more active parishioners belong to more than one of these groups. Mrs Wiseman, for example, who runs the Women's League, is also a prominent member of the

Legion of Mary, and so on. And then some of the organisations cover more than one parish, and meetings are not necessarily held here in Droitwich.'

'Right, Father, in that case, would you draw up a short list of the main areas in which we can meet the business end of the parish? - if I may so phrase it with all respect to the clergy! We should like to start as soon as possible.'

'I've got a funeral in half an hour,' Fr Gabriel said. 'Can I phone a list through to you later on this morning or this afternoon?'

Wickfield conceded that there would be no problem there, since, as virtually all the parish groups met in the evenings, with Saturdays excluded altogether, they could not start until the following day.

The first sampling of parish life, the youth group, came that Sunday night. Wickfield and Spooner went along to mingle with the youths, who ranged in age from fourteen to twenty. Although all sorts of activities were organised week by week, the emphasis at the 'club', held in the parish hall, was on the social needs of Catholic teenagers. They had hardly stepped foot inside the door when Miss Kylie Bradford seized Spooner by the arm and told him she was going to introduce him to members of the club. First she took him to an older man.

'This,' she told him, 'is Gavin, who likes to think he's in charge.' Then followed a series of spotty boys and loud girls with names like Ross and Alana, Yoslene and Marlon, with all of whom Spooner shook hands or nodded in acknowledgment. The main item of business that evening was putting the final touches to a concert the youth were giving the elderly of the parish the following Saturday afternoon. 'Concert' was, as quickly became apparent to the two detectives, a slightly elevated word for what was likely to transpire, but they could not deny the enthusiasm with which the young people plotted the succession of turns and discussed the provision of refreshments, the raffle and the spot prizes. Typical of the detectives' conversations was one with Tim, a youth of sixteen in his final year of O-levels.

'Do you come every week?' Wickfield asked him.

'Oh, yes,' said Tim. 'It's good fun, and I meet my mates.'

'But presumably you meet them all week at school?'

'Yes, but here we haven't got teachers hanging around, and in any case there's people I don't see at school.'

'Let me ask you about the parish. Do you go to church on Sundays?'

'Yes, generally.'

'What do you think of the Mass in English?'

'It's all right, I suppose.'

'Has it made a big difference to you?'

'No, not really, it's all pretty incomprehensible anyway, isn't it?'

'So what do you go for?'

'Habit. Keep the family company. I dunno, what does anybody go to church for?'

'Did you get on with Fr Wilfred?'

'All right, I suppose. We didn't really see much of him, not in here, anyway. It was always Fr Gabriel who came in.'

'Were you shocked to hear Fr Wilfred had been murdered?'

'Yes, of course. You could easily spend a whole lifetime without knowing anyone who'd been murdered.'

'Any ideas on the subject?'

'No, not really. We've talked about it, of course – '

'And have you come up with any suggestions?'

'Not really. You see, we don't know exactly what happened. We know he was stabbed as he was hearing confessions, that's all. Could have been any tramp or madman wandering the streets; just dropped in for a bit of fun, couldn't it?'

Further conversation was prevented by the arrival of Miss Kylie Bradford, who sashayed up purposefully, having presumably filled Sergeant Spooner's ears with whatever it was she had to say to him.

'It's so exciting seeing two real detectives here,' she spluttered. 'I can hardly believe it.'

'Yes, well, it's a very serious matter, you know, murder.'

'How far have you got with your investigation – Inspector?' she asked with a provocative grin. Tim listened in.

'If you mean, Have we made an arrest? the answer is no, we haven't. I should hardly be here tonight if we had, should I?'

'Who are your suspects, Inspector? You can tell me!'

'No, I can't, Young Lady, and you know I can't. If it comes to that, you were there that evening: we have to consider the possibility that *you* could have done it.'

'Me? Me, Inspector? What would I be doing going round murdering old priests?'

'You might have thought he was an obstacle to the modernisation of the Church.'

'But we all thought that! That's no reason to murder the old man.'

'You're not very respectful, are you, Miss Bradford?'

'I don't mean any harm by it, but if the Church is to attract young people, make them feel at home, give them some sort of inspiration for living, doesn't it have a duty to give us priests who can relate to us, speak on our wave-length, bring the Church into the twentieth century? Fr Tarbuck was old-fashioned and out of touch. He made no effort to meet us on our own ground. Fr Gabriel at least tried to talk to us about the changes proposed by some council in Rome that met recently. I want to be a good Catholic, but it's all still so stuffy.'

'Stuffy? In what way?'

'Let me give you some examples, Inspector. Fr Gabriel has told us that the Church authorities, God bless their cotton socks, are contemplating changing the ruling on birth control. About time! But I bet you they don't. I bet you anything you like. And what about married priests, priests with families who know what it's all about? What about women priests? Why aren't women – half the human race, for heaven's sake – allowed to make any decisions? What about prayers we can understand? "Our Father, who art in heaven, hallowed be thy name": what sort of English is that? What about all those funny robes the priests wear? Why can't they dress soberly and simply? What's all this with receiving communion on the tongue? I don't get it. And little wafers instead of proper bread? And whatever happened to the wine?'

'Yes, well, let me interrupt you there, Young Lady,' said Wickfield. 'You've made your point, but you must realise, I'm sure you do, that like any other institution, the Church moves very slowly. You need to have a bit more patience.'

'Patience! And in the meantime, young people are leaving the Church in droves. They're living together, not bothering to get married in church, not having their kids baptised. Priests are leaving, and my mum says it often seems to be the more thoughtful ones who go.'

'Do you think any of this has anything to do with Fr Wilfred's death?'

'How do I know? But I told you before, Inspector, he got in the way of people who want change. Isn't that a good enough reason for murder? It isn't, in my book, but I can't answer for everyone, can I?' she asked archly.

The following day, Spooner, obeying orders, had drawn up a profile of the deceased, combining the archdiocesan file with the reminiscences of Miss Tarbuck, whom sorrow had subdued to the point of being tolerably affable with him when he met her at her hotel on that Saturday afternoon over tea and buttered tea-cakes. (Would that all his assignments were so agreeable!) This is what he came up with:

Wilfred John Tarbuck, born 3 June 1900, second son and third child of William Tarbuck, newsagent, and his wife Hilda, of 15 Glover Street, West Bromwich. George Betts Primary School, West End Avenue, Smethwick, 1905-1911. Cotton College, Oakmoor, Stoke-on-Trent, 1911-1918. Oscott College, Sutton Coldfield, 1919-1925. Ordained priest 13 June 1925.

First appointment: curate at St Francis, Hunter's Road, Handsworth, 1925.

Then curate successively at St Patrick, Dudley Road, Birmingham, 1926-1928; Sacred Heart and St Margaret Mary, Witton Road, Aston, 1928-1931; and St Patrick, Blue Lane, Walsall, 1931-1934;

Then parish priest at St Margaret Mary, Perry Common, 1934-1946; and finally at Sacred Heart and St Catherine of Alexandria, Worcester Road, Droitwich 1946-1968.

Despite his years at Cotton College (the junior seminary), Wilfred did not immediately decide to pursue his studies for the priesthood but became instead a clerk at Avery's in Smethwick, living at home. He applied to attend Oscott in June of 1919 and was admitted, on the advice of his parish priest, in September of that year. His studies were normal and effective, and there was apparently no hesitation on his part in accepting the various offices leading up to subdiaconate, diaconate and priesthood.

His career [NB not sure whether priests have a 'career', exactly!] path was quite normal. It began with some years as a curate, learning the job, with the experience of different parishes and associated institutions. Thus his first parish contained two primary schools, a maternity home, a premature baby unit and two nursing homes; his second a primary school, a comprehensive school and two hospitals; his fourth a primary school, a convent and again two hospitals. When the time was ripe, he was appointed, first, to a small(ish) one-horse parish, and then to Droitwich, with responsibility for a curate. It seems probable that, had he lived, he would have continued at Droitwich, retiring in due course to a convent or an old priests' home to live out his final years.

His ministry was characterised by adherence to clerical conventions – so, for example, he would always wear his clerical collar when outside his presbytery - a zealous approach to his sacerdotal duties and a slightly open attitude to his parishioners. At deanery meetings he spoke little but was acknowledged by his peers to be theologically well-informed.

His hobbies included a round of golf once a week, tending the parish garden (if there was one), reading and ecclesiastical architecture.

In manner he could come across as stiff or staid, but he could be jovial, and his sense of humour, while refined and above coarseness, was not above flippancy when occasion offered. His habits were abstemious: he rarely indulged in alcohol, although he did smoke quite heavily, and he was not known to party. He did not need a housekeeper to remind him that his cassock had gravy down the front or that his shoes were scuffed. Towards his curates he was considered not exactly harsh, but certainly very firm, since he had clear ideas as to what was suitable in a clergyman and what not.

His relationship to clergymen of other persuasions tended not to be cordial. He generally refused invitations to attend services in Anglican and Protestant Churches and Non-Conformist chapels and was therefore sometimes considered 'standoffish' or 'superior'. His sermons were serious and decently crafted, but because he read them out in something of a monotone, the congregation were respectful rather than enthusiastic. No one could fault his ministry to the sick and dying or the correctness with which he approached his duties in schools: he was not frightened of the young, even though he may not have lit their inner fires.

His health was good, apart from a tendency in his last months to serious forgetfulness, for which he had consulted his general practitioner, as he apparently feared it might indicate approaching mental decline.

Wickfield decided to postpone discussion of this document until such time as they had completed their circuit of the parish (as it were) and had a wider context in which to consider it. It did not look promising, in the sense that it did not seem to contain much that would explain a murderous hatred. Fr Wilfred's life seemed to have been solid, prosaic from one point of view, yet certainly worthy. One never knew, however.

The detectives' tour of the parish groups continued with the Third World Aid meeting in the church hall on the Tuesday. Eight members of the parish, chaired by a very unPecksniffian architect called George Roundway, were present. The meeting's format, they were told, never varied: prayers, business, refreshments, both in chronological order and in descending order of importance. Wickfield had taken the trouble to prime his assistant with the following words:

'We are here as observers and listeners. What are we observing? what are we listening for? You may well ask! No, no, I'm joking. We're interested not so much in how the parish functions on the ground, the work it does, as in the personalities who do the work, in so far as it's possible to tease the two apart. We are to be receivers of vibrations, if that is not too pompous a phrase. On the other hand, there is nothing to stop us having words with the participants afterwards in our search for meaning!'

After the initial prayers, the chairman welcomed their two visitors, explaining that they were there not to make an arrest – at least he hoped not! – but to get a feel for the parish, since neither of them was a Catholic, and they were still wondering why a parishioner should wish to dispose of a worthy and venerable parish priest. He also apologised for Fr Gabriel's absence. The curate generally looked in, he explained, but that evening he was engaged on final preparations for Fr Wilfred's funeral on the morrow. The business of the meeting focused on a Bring and Buy to be held on the first Saturday morning of March – only just over a fortnight away! – and Wickfield and Spooner were interested to see that Mr Thomas Foynes, school laboratory assistant, was clearly a prominent member of the group, since he had much to say and was listened to without demur. The discussion naturally focused on maximising both the donations and the attendance, and much was said on exceeding the sum raised the previous year and what measures the group might take to improve on last year's organisation. Over tea and biscuits afterwards, Wickfield took the opportunity to have a word with the chairman. George Roundway was, as his name intimated beyond all logic – a bit like owners resembling their dogs - a rotund little man, with a large bald head and bristling moustache and trousers that, hanging below his waist, necessarily fell in unsightly folds on his shoes. He was jovial and amiable and gave himself no airs.

'Mr Roundway,' Wickfield began, 'may I ask how long you have been chairman of this group?'

'Two years, Inspector, since its inception, in fact.'

'Was it you who set it up?'

'No, not really, it was the previous curate, Fr David -- he was moved on to another parish after disagreements with Fr Wilfred, we understand - but he asked for lay volunteers, and I volunteered. You see, he told us it was a response to Vatican II, which wanted to increase the part played by the laity in parish life and to deepen the Church's work in building up the world.'

'He actually used that phrase?'

'What phrase?'

'"Building up the world"?'

'Oh, yes, he quoted one of the council documents, something like, "All should work together to build up the world in genuine peace", and that's been a sort of motto for us ever since. You see, he explained to us that for centuries specific action targeted at improving the lot of the world's poor had slipped down the Church's agenda in favour of other, more specifically "churchy" activities, and that the council was keen to redress the balance by raising its status.'

'Admirable,' commented Wickfield. 'Sorry,' he added, 'I speak out of turn as an outsider.'

'Not at all, Inspector: absolutely no apology needed. If you are impressed, the council's efforts to improve the mission and the face of the Church have succeeded.'

'May I ask where Fr Wilfred stood on this?'

'He was not very keen, to be honest. He didn't exactly try to block the formation of this group, but he made it plain that he didn't agree with it and that we should be much better employed on our knees in church.'

'Is there any opposition to you still in the parish ranks?'

'Oh, I daresay there is, but there's room for all sorts, and I see no need to fall out with anybody over it. If someone prefers to sing in the choir or arrange flowers for the church, so be it. The group is well supported by the parish when we put on something like a Bring and Buy, so enough people agree with our aims to make the group viable, and we're not really asking for or expecting more than that. Fr Gabriel is helpful: he has occasionally used the end of a sermon to highlight our work, and he pops in to our meetings when he can.'

Five

*F*r Wilfred's funeral took place on the following morning. The archbishop himself said the Mass, assisted by a large number of clergy who wished to concelebrate. The church, though commodious, was full, partly because the priest's death had aroused much interest in the town. Local dignitaries and non-Catholic clergy had been invited. Wickfield and Spooner, having asked to have seats reserved where they would be unobtrusive but in a position to view the proceedings, were seated in the front row of the small gallery at the back of the church. Nothing untoward occurred. The archbishop's sermon focussed on the three points: Fr Wilfred's outstanding years of service to the priesthood, the uncertainties of life, and the tide of lawlessness that threatened to engulf British society in the wake of the current permissive moral sense. It was not well-wrought but came across as sincere, reflective and spiritual.

Fr Wilfred was to be buried in the cemetery at Oscott College, and Wickfield and Spooner chose to attend. First amongst the mourners were the deceased's sister and one or two other people of a similar age whom Wickfield took to be the other sibling and family members. Then came the archdiocesan clergy, in cassock, surplice and stole, representatives of the Droitwich parish, suitably turned out, and finally everybody else. The day was overcast and chilly; those assembled were in any case sombre. As the celebrant moved through the final sequence of the ritual – the blessing of the grave, the incensing of the body, the singing of Zachariah's Canticle, the final sign of the cross over the deceased – Wickfield felt a nudge in his side and turned to find Mr Thomas Foynes at his elbow.

'That's him,' said Foynes, nodding in the direction of a head two or three paces in front of them in the crowd of mourners.

'*Fac, quaesumus, Domine, hanc cum servo tuo defuncto misericordiam …*'

'Who?'

' *… ut, sicut hic eum vera fides junxit fidelium turmis …* '

'The man sitting in the front row of the church Fr Wilfred spoke to on his way to hear confessions.'

' *… ita illic eum tua miseratio societ angelicis choris.* '

When he was sure he had correctly identified the person indicated by Thomas Foynes, he said,

'Good, thanks,' and turned to Spooner to convey the news.

The funeral service came to an end with the casting of clods on to the lowered coffin, and the crowd began to disperse, mainly in silence and sombrely. Their quarry looked surprised, as well he might, to find a detective inspector on one side of him and a detective sergeant on the other, just as he had thoughts only for leaving the cemetery and going about his business.

'Could we have a quick word, Sir?' Spooner said in his ear, at the same time discreetly showing his identification card. 'Worcestershire CID,' he added by way of reinforcement.

'We understand you were at the Sacred Heart Church last Thursday, Sir, just before the time of Benediction.'

'Yes, possibly I was. Why do you ask?'

'Well, Sir, you will know that we are investigating Fr Wilfred's murder, and we are trying to contact people in the church at the time who might have seen something. Our information is that you were one of the last people to speak to him.'

'Maybe I was, but, being in the front row, I couldn't very well see anything of what was happening in the church, could I?'

'May I ask what you spoke to Fr Wilfred about?'

'No, you may not, Sergeant. That is entirely my business.'

'Look, Sir, this is a murder investigation, and we need your cooperation. I must ask you to give us your name and address, and we may need to contact you later.'

That was as much as the detectives achieved with that particular witness – or perhaps more properly that *soi-disant* non-witness. Wickfield decided that the man's apparent role in the events of Thursday evening did not warrant holding him at the end of a funeral service; they would catch up with him later.

That same evening, the weekly meeting of the St Vincent de Paul Society took place in the home of one of its members, a Mr Talbot Coleman, and both detectives attended. Before all the eight members were assembled, Mr Coleman had time to sketch in the role of the SVP in the parish. His large moustache trembled with every word he spoke.

'The SVP,' he explained, 'is an international organisation but parish-based. We are what is called a Conference operating in Droitwich, and it would take me a long time to outline all we do! The Society takes its inspiration from the work of St Vincent de Paul, the seventeenth-century French priest, as you might have guessed, and focuses on the needy in our locality. We try to help out with advice, furniture, money, accommodation, whatever is required at the time; we run disability projects, soup kitchens, children's camps, furniture stores and so on – not all here in Droitwich, of course, but in the bigger cities. The emphasis is always on visiting and personal contact.'

'How do people contact you?' Spooner asked.

'Well, they're almost invariably referred to us by the clergy. Either the person who needs a bit of a hand goes to the priest, or the priest identifies a need in the course of his parish visiting, and the person and the SVP are brought together. It is endless work, as the pit of suffering and necessity is, I'm afraid, even in affluent Britain, bottomless.'

'And in this parish, if I've understood correctly, it's Fr Gabriel who does the parish visiting.'

'Well, it is, but Fr Wilfred is – or perhaps I had better say was, poor man – very supportive. You mustn't think that just because he didn't get around much he had no care for the poor! On the other hand, Fr Gabriel took a special interest in our work and often followed up our visits with visits of his own.'

By then the group – the 'Conference' – was assembled, and the meeting began. It had been agreed not to cancel the meeting because of the bereavement in the parish: the poor were with them always! The main item on the agenda was the establishment of a Community Shop in Birmingham which the group had been asked to support. Talbot Coleman proved an able and affable chairman, despite the erratic comments of Mr Christopher Ross, whose commitment to the cause was not in doubt but whose personal interventions left something to be desired in the way of tact and grace of expression. One of his less tactful interventions went somewhat as follows.

'Look, Talbot, you can't just ignore Fr Tarbuck's death, you know, as if it had never happened. The man's gone, and I move that we use the occasion to promote the work of the Conference.'

'What exactly had you in mind, Chris?'

Ross looked round the group, taking in the two visitors as well.

'Between ourselves,' he said, 'I hope Fr Gabriel is made parish priest –`

'Impossible!' said a voice.

'Much too young and inexperienced!' said another.

'Hear, hear!' said a third.

' – because he would improve our image in the parish overnight. Fr Wilfred was too much involved in churchy things, but what we need to be doing as a Catholic parish is getting out into the community and giving practical expression to our concern. What we want is not Benediction and rosary and all that pious stuff but help on the ground!'

'Perhaps the two go hand in hand,' the chairman said pacifically, 'but perhaps we should wait until we see who is appointed in Fr Wilfred's place before we start any capers.'

A disgruntled but unruffled Christopher Ross fell silent. The meeting clearly had a lot of sympathy both for the man and for his point of view. After a little more conversation and a final prayer, Talbot's wife June brought in a tray of mugs and the business part of the meeting was over.

On the Thursday evening, two parish meetings were held, and Wickfield and Spooner divided their forces. Sergeant Spooner attended a meeting of the Catholic Women's League. He felt very out of place as the only man amongst fourteen or fifteen women, but they did not seem put out once Mrs Wiseman had explained the purpose of his presence.

'We shall choose to ignore you, dear,' she said, and the others laughed. 'No, no, what I mean is, you are most welcome, but we are going to hold our meeting as if you weren't here. That's what you want, isn't it, if I understood your inspector properly?'

After the meeting, at which a number of quite disparate items were discussed, Spooner found himself chatting to Mrs Veronica Green over tea and cakes.

'We're already acquainted,' Mrs Green told Mrs Wiseman. 'You see, I happened to be in church the night Fr Wilfred died.' Mrs Wiseman drifted off.

'Could you just tell me a bit about the League?' the sergeant asked Mrs Green.

'Well, Sergeant, tonight, as you know, we discussed some new arrangements for a crèche at Worcester Crown Court, supplying a little more assistance to the catechetics teachers during the main Sunday Mass, and our next Sale of Work – that gives you a fair view of some of the things we get up to, but we could equally well have been talking about a study weekend, or house-visits to the sick, support for CAFOD at an approaching flag-day or a day of recollection for the women of the parish.'

'That's quite a range,' Spooner said in admiration.

'Well, we try to mix improving our spiritual lives with direct action in the community. We women are so much better at juggling several things at once than you men.' This was said with a knowing smile.

'I bet Fr Wilfred was a bit afraid of you, wasn't he?' hazarded Spooner.

'Yes, probably. I don't think he knew quite what to make of us.'

'You seem a very lively group, if I may say so.'

'Oh, yes, Fr Gabriel's made a big difference to our status in the parish. Before he came, people looked at us a bit askance, as if

55

somehow we were trying to usurp the clergy's role in encouraging spirituality and looking at so many aspects of parish life. But Fr Gabriel explained to us that that was exactly what Vatican II intended. He also added that the council was a bit afraid of women but made a special effort to include one unmistakable statement to the effect that it desired women to take a much more prominent role in the Church's apostolate.'

'Could I just ask a slightly different question: have you any idea why someone might dislike Fr Wilfred so much as to wish to murder him?'

'Sergeant, it could be anyone, not necessarily a parishioner at all. The presbytery gets all sorts at the door: down-and-outs, tramps, gypsies, the homeless, people with mental health problems, you name it. The church is open all day every day. It could be just anyone.'

Wickfield, meanwhile, was attending a meeting of the choir in church, where the low temperature allowed to persist for most of the week outside service times was boosted a little for comfort's sake. The choir consisted of three sopranos, two altos, two tenors and a bass, under the baton of the redoubtable Mrs Gwynneth Fox. They tried one piece of polyphony each week, and a Mass on major feast-days, but their main function was to sustain the singing of the hymns and such like: not a substitute for the congregation, but a prop. However, Wickfield saw little point in attending the choir practice, whereat he would have no opportunity to hear the members expressing thoughts and feelings about the parish, opting instead, with manful commitment to duty, to join the choir at the Doverdale Arms for a little liquid refreshment after the labours of the practice. Mrs Fox proved to be every bit the forceful personality that her position on the (metaphorical) rostrum had suggested, and she was not slow to impart to the inspector her philosophy as choir-mistress.

'You see, Inspector, I happen to believe that the Second Vatican Council was naïve. Fr Gabriel's predecessor, who regrettably didn't last long in the parish – some brush-up with Fr Wilfred, I think – told us that the Council fathers expressed a preference for Gregorian chant at public worship, but we agreed that the average English parish just wouldn't take to that, so we opted instead for the Council's second and third preferences: polyphony and congregational singing: according to Fr Gabriel, the Council's very words were, "Let the voices of the faithful ring out". Now the bishops apparently also encouraged composers to come up with new material more in keeping with the times, so we decided we would make a special point of learning new hymns, and that way we have achieved what I consider to be a very proper balance: we offer a piece of polyphony, to satisfy the demands of tradition and the canons of liturgical beauty, and we encourage the congregation in fresh hymns to keep their interest. Now what do you say to that?' This was the first time she had paused for breath in her little exposition of the principles behind her management of the choir.

'Admirable, Mrs Fox, but you haven't mentioned Fr Wilfred's attitude to all this. He *was* the parish priest, you know.'

'Oh, I know all that, but all he wanted was to continue the old and familiar hymns. You see – ' here she dropped her voice to a whisper – 'he didn't really approve of women singing in church. Such an old fuddy-duddy.'

'Are you saying he stood in the way of progress?'

'Well, only in the sense that he never encouraged change himself. He seemed fairly content for his curates to foster change, within reason.'

At some point, three of the members, including Mrs Fox, left the public house, crying duty to their families, and Inspector Wickfield found himself sitting next to Miss Warren, to whom he had listened but not spoken before. A slightly different aspect of the old lady emerged, not at all to her detriment, as he reported to Spooner later. Her physical limitations were not so apparent when she was sitting, and there was a sparkle in her old eyes that belied her years.

'Your choir-mistress seems fairly go-ahead,' Wickfield began conversationally. 'I suppose she carries the choir with her by sheer force of personality!'

'Well, that's not quite fair on us, Inspector. We may look to be dyed-in-the-wool reactionaries, but you know, we're not really. Take me, for instance. I'm in my seventy-third year, and I've never married or had children, but I can appreciate that the young don't want the old hymns that used to satisfy us and our parents. Can I tell you what I'm reading at the moment? - d'Azeglio's *Ricordi*. He was a great Italian painter, novelist and statesman of nineteenth-century Italy - you've undoubtedly heard of him, Inspector - and I am enjoying his memoirs immensely. When he was twelve, he asked his father whether the family were noble, and do you know what his father said? Remember that his father was a marquis and his mother the daughter of a marquis. His father said, "*Sarai nobile, se sarai virtuoso*": you will be noble if you are virtuous. However, that's not what I wished to quote to you. At one point in his adolescence he met Count Castellalfero, the Sardinian ambassador to the Tuscan court, and he comments – and the words have stayed with me – "He was not angry with the young because he was no longer young". That surely demonstrates great wisdom, Inspector, and it says much about d'Azeglio that he thought it worth including in his memoirs. That's a long-winded way of saying that while I liked Fr Wilfred and sympathised with his stodgy ways, I'm very glad to belong to a choir which is bringing something fresh to the parish.'

'I'll be quite honest with you, Miss Warren. We can't understand why anyone should wish to murder Fr Wilfred. He may have lacked enthusiasm for new ways, but he seems to have been harmless and to have been tolerated even if not widely loved in the parish. That's what we're picking up from talking to parishioners.'

'Well, I can't understand it either, Inspector, but religion can lead some people to unbelievable lengths of fanatic stupidity, and in that I'm not telling you anything you don't know already: I can see at a glance that you're wise in the world's ways. Many leaders, religious and otherwise, have been assassinated because some unbalanced person thought their removal would improve matters, whereas often the vacuum is filled by someone worse. If even popes can get themselves murdered, why not parish priests?'

'You haven't anyone in mind, I suppose?'

'Gracious, no, Inspector: I speak in general terms only. I don't for one minute imagine that religious fanatics are at work in Droitwich, smoothing the way for innovation by engaging in dastardly acts, but surely someone out there is on the rampage.'

After this final session at parish groups, Wickfield and Spooner sat down to hold, as it were, a post mortem. They had met back at the station to install themselves in the inspector's office, and when both were comfortably seated and supplied with bottles of beer (for the sergeant) and a pot of tea (for the inspector), Wickfield began by asking Spooner about his meeting with the CWL, while he in turn outlined his evening with the choir. He then scribbled on a scrap of paper drawn from an untidy heap on his desk the main events in their investigation to date.

'Right,' he said, 'this is what we've got.

- Fr Wilfred is done to death in his confessional, Thursday evening.

- Only five people went to confession that evening, and of those five only three used the altar end of the confessional, the end which would have enabled a penitent to stab the priest in his right side: Mrs Green, Miss Bradford and Miss Warren. This detail may or may not be relevant.

- We interviewed all five on the Friday evening, and all seemed honest and innocent!

- On the Saturday we met Fr Gabriel again and discussed 'tensions' in the parish.

- On Sunday and Tuesday evenings respectively, we attended the Youth Club and a meeting of the Third World Aid group.

- On Monday, you kindly and efficiently draw up a profile of the deceased.

- On Wednesday we attended Fr Wilfred's funeral, and an unknown visitor to the church the previous Thursday evening was one of the mourners. That evening we sat in on a meeting of the SVP.

- Then earlier tonight we attended meetings of the CWL and the choir. We've been busy, have we not? but I'm not sure where it's all got us.'

Wickfield paused at this point, apparently at a loss for further comment. Spooner coughed.

'Yes, Sergeant?' Wickfield looked up.

'I've been thinking, Sir.'

'I should hope so: that's what you're paid for.'

'You understand this is only an idea, Sir.'

'Yes, yes, get on with it. Why are you hesitating?'

Spooner swallowed self-consciously and paused to pour some more beer into his glass.

'Well, you see, Sir, what if we disregard the penitents?'

'Disregard the penitents? What can you mean? What are you trying to say?'

'Well, I'm not disregarding them altogether, Sir, just sidelining them for a moment while we consider another possibility.'

'I see. In other words, you've got a better idea than mine.'

'You're not making this easy for me, Sir.'

'Spooner, for heaven's sake, you've known me for long enough now, surely, to know that no idea is irreformable, whether I come out with it or you do. Right, let's put the penitents aside for the moment. Who's left?'

'Would it have been possible for a person in the church to have walked slowly down the side-aisle past the confessional, as if to leave the church, reach into the confessional through the curtain – remember, the doors were open – stab the priest and move on without being noticed?'

'OK, but why has no one mentioned this person?'

'Perhaps they have, perhaps he or she is one of the people we know about, perhaps the mysterious man in the front row. The church is a big one, the lighting probably not brilliant for a small service; people were deep in their prayers, like Mrs Green, or in their prayer-books, like Miss Warren, not looking round them. This person strolls down in silence, makes a movement at the door of the confessional which passes unnoticed or is interpreted as the conveyance of a quiet greeting to the priest and walks out of the church.'

'Right. Then that person would have to be left-handed to have delivered a blow on the priest's right side.'

'Yes, he or she might well have thought that that would not betray them, or they deliberately used their left hand to confuse us.'

'Yes, I'm afraid we're easily confused at the moment. What we need to do to test your idea, then, is to recreate the events of last Thursday night: assemble all the people we know about and get them to run through the half-hour of confessions again, with the same lighting, at the same time of day and so on. I wonder why I never thought of that before. OK, we'll get that organised tomorrow. Well done, Sergeant. The other question to consider is motive: has our attendance at five parish groups got us anywhere? What are your impressions of the parish?'

'For me, Sir, the personalities of the priests reflect two different schools of thought which are going to be difficult to reconcile, except that's a problem for the archbishop, not for us. The parish seems to be split between the old guard and the progressives, largely along lines of age, I think. Has Fr Wilfred been caught in the mincer and got ground out of existence?'

'What a turn of phrase you have, Sergeant! Just take us through the meetings, will you, and add in your own comments about Fr Tarbuck as a person.'

'OK, Sir. Youth Club. Serious young people, keen to make a difference, and agreed that Fr Tarbuck was not much good to them. If young Miss Bradford is typical, they're too dizzy to put a murder plot together. On the other hand, they perhaps have the daring and the nonchalance to attempt it. Next, Third World Aid. They had little to thank Fr Tarbuck for, seemingly, but they are able to carry out their work unhampered, and they all seem too sober to be criminal-minded. Perhaps I'm a poor judge of character.'

'We probably all are, Sergeant: don't let it get you down!' Spooner glanced up from his notes momentarily and gave a brief grin.

'Thirdly, the SVP and our friend Mr Ross. Committed relievers of poverty. If the chairman is anyone to go by, the murder of Fr Tarbuck is far from their minds, unless one of the members is so fanatical as to contemplate murder in the perceived interests of the poor. To find *that* out we'd have to interview all the members, and we still, like the world's economists put end to end, wouldn't reach a conclusion.'

'Quite!'

'In fourth place, the CWL, where I felt extremely conspicuous, not to say embarrassed. Perhaps a more mature man would have been more at ease,' he said, looking up at the inspector.

'Keep going, my lad, you're doing fine!'

'Intense women, no shrinking violets there, but murder? There did not seem to be a deep love of their parish priest on the one hand, and there did seem to be a welcome for the council's encouragement of women's work on the other. A woman would certainly be capable of murder, just as a man would, but the group seem to have found sufficient support in Fr Gabriel. And so, finally, to our last parish group, the choir, where you spent most of your time – with respect, of course, Sir – sitting in a pub chatting up intelligent old ladies.' Wickfield smirked. 'Your account of the experience gives no indication of murderous intent, but perhaps lurking somewhere in the background is an uncompromising extremist intent on pulling down the preconciliar Church and all it stood for!'

'You have a way with words, Sergeant! And what about the priest's personal life?'

'It seems to have been unexciting but exemplary, not a life to get worked up about. He was a loyal and sincere man, competent, prayerful, efficient, not perhaps very dynamic, but surely not, on the basis of his life alone, an object of murder.'

'Your conclusion therefore is?'

'That he died not for who he was but for what he stood for.'

'Excellent, thank you for all that, Spooner. I think that before we can take our theories any further, we need to follow up your suggestion of a reconstruction. That'll be our task for tomorrow.'

Six

*T*he first step was to locate the mysterious stranger so that he could be 'invited' to participate in the reconstruction of the previous Thursday evening's dramatic events. Wickfield admitted to himself that the denomination 'mysterious stranger', conferred on him by Spooner in one of his lighter moments, was unnecessarily sensational, misleading and in fact inapt. There was nothing particularly mysterious about an honest and worthy citizen who chose to say a few prayers at the front of a church and then declined to announce his business to the first policeman who came along. He sent Spooner along to Kenilworth to make contact and to express the hope that he could see his way to attend the reconstruction that very evening. The man had given his name as Damian Fay and his address as 2 Crackley Lane, Kenilworth, and Spooner enjoyed his little jaunt thirty miles into Warwickshire in search of a possible murderer. He turned off the Coventry Road and almost immediately found the short drive leading to a detached house, No.2, surrounded by trees and a small garden. The house was comfortably sized but not extravagant, and well-kept. There was no one at home. The sergeant therefore walked round to No.4, and there an elderly lady was kind enough to point him in the direction of the castle, where he had only to ask for the administrator. After a short journey, and after parking his car, he found himself standing before the immense ruins, but instead of fumbling in his pocket for the admittance fee, he flourished his card and was eventually invited to follow an attendant into the presence of the administrator, whose office was not in the castle itself but in the gatehouse.

Damian Fay was a man nearer fifty than forty, Spooner judged, well-preserved, even vigorous, with smooth black hair flat to his skull, black eyes and a determined face. When Spooner announced his name and rank, recognition but also displeasure made itself visible, but the man's manner was courteous enough: 'coldly polite' would perhaps express the matter. Spooner explained his business briefly, and Mr Fay had the grace to ask him to take a seat. The room was a quite splendid beamed apartment on the first floor of the gatehouse, with mullioned and leaded windows looking fore and aft. Many books were scattered around, along with estate charts, maps, lists of employees, spikes of invoices, box-files and 'useful addresses'. Spooner, determined not to antagonise the administrator, adopted his most ingratiating manner.

'You see, Sir,' he said, 'we need you there tonight just in case you saw something no one else did. The purpose of the reconstruction is to jog people's memories so that they can come forward with details that haven't yet been made known to us.'

'I told you last week, Sergeant, that because I was sitting at the front, I couldn't see anything of what went on in the nave, and in any case I was only in the church for a few minutes.'

'Yes, Sir, but as you came in and as you went out, you may well have seen something that is significant, if only we knew of it.'

'Well, I didn't. Nothing unusual was going on that I noticed: just a few people saying their prayers or lighting candles. I'm sorry I can't be of any help, Sergeant, so if you'll excuse me … '

'At the very least, Sir, you may be able to corroborate other witnesses about who was where and who was doing what. We're not finding it easy to discover how the murder was committed, let alone who was responsible, and if you're not there, I'm not sure how useful the reconstruction will be.'

When Mr Fay made no comment, Spooner continued his theme.

'Look, Sir, a venerable priest is attacked in his own church when people are about who might have seen something. We need everybody there tonight.'

Fay stayed silent, nibbling at his thumb and cogitating.

'Sergeant, I am relying on your absolute discretion. I know that your inspector will have to be told, but I hope that's as far as it'll go. I was in Droitwich last week to see my father.'

When he paused, Spooner gave an encouraging cough and looked squarely at his man.

'Fr Wilfred was my father.'

Spooner was stunned. He had never imagined such a disclosure, and for a short while he could not find the words to utter.

'I see, Sir,' he eventually managed. 'That puts a quite different complexion on things. I wonder whether you would like to tell me about it.'

'Look, Sergeant, would you mind if I got myself a cup of coffee? Can I get you one at the same time?'

'Yes, thank you, that would be welcome.'

'Milk? sugar?'

Fay disappeared for a few minutes and returned with two plastic cups of coffee and a small packet of biscuits each. After a few minutes' silence, Fay began his narrative.

'I was born in 1918, when my father was eighteen. He was then working as a clerk at Avery's in Smethwick, where his job was in the department that had responsibility for the management of all the company's files. He had not long left school and was still living at home. A woman in the same department was called Ann, Ann Fay, and she and my father had a relationship which resulted in my birth. My mother was eighteen at the time. Of course her pregnancy and motherhood put paid to her job, and she left her small room in Smethwick to return to her parents' house. Eventually she was able to return to work when her mother could look after me during the day. Now I'm not sure of the details, and both my parents are dead, so there's nobody left to enlighten me, but this is what I've always understood. My father's parents, Hilda and William, who were very anxious for my father to proceed to the priesthood, had a conference with my mother's parents to which my parents were invited. Neither of my parents could positively affirm that they thought marriage would be the best option or that it would work: they both knew that they were young, too young, and that they had been activated by emotion rather than by reasoned love. The conference was apparently amicable and constructive and concluded with a sort of compromise. My father's parents would contribute to the child's upbringing until their son could add his ha'porth out of his meagre earnings as a priest, and Ann was free to marry anybody else if she so chose, without strings. So in due course my father left for the seminary, and I was brought up by my mother and maternal grandparents in Smethwick. Life was not too bad. Between them, my two sets of grandparents and my mother earned or contributed enough to fund a modest lower middle-class life-style, and if I missed my father, I knew no better.'

'Your father must have contacted you at some stage,' Spooner said.

'I'm coming to that, Sergeant. At some point in his seminary career, presumably towards the end of it when he was required to commit himself to the priesthood for good, my father must have gone to the archbishop and confessed, and the archbishop was apparently very understanding. The seminary authorities gave a good account of his progress, and the archbishop was happy for him to proceed to ordination. The archbishop also said that it was not good for me to have no contact with my father. My father was therefore appointed as curate to parishes close enough to Smethwick to make visits possible, and when I was six or seven, he began to visit weekly on his days off. The archbishop allowed limited contact between my parents but expressed the fear that too much would lead to a resumption of the liaison, and my father respected that. Since I was at school, my father and I met after school for the evening. He would take me to the cinema, or for a walk in the park, or perhaps to a museum, and we would have tea together.'

'Were they happy times, Sir?' Spooner asked sympathetically.

'Yes, I suppose so. I can't complain. My mother was a very good mother, and my grandparents helped out a lot – both sets.'

'Did your mother never marry?'

'She did, when I was eighteen, a man called Dominic Flint. Now he and I didn't hit it off particularly, and in any case I was ready to leave home. Thereafter I saw less and less of my mother, which was always a sorrow to me, and of course my father was even less welcome in the house than I was. There was never a row or major bust-up, we just never got on, and I respected my mother's need to enjoy a life of her own. My mother died in 1963, and so I never see Dominic at all now.'

'What sort of a man was your father?'

'Hard to say, in a way, because he wasn't the sort of person to grind on about his own thoughts and feelings, but he struck me as being perfectly happy in his priesthood. He was a conscientious man, content to fulfil his duties and without ambition. Does that make him sound dull? Perhaps he was. He was also rather - how shall I express this? - staid; he didn't take kindly to innovation. Through his forties and fifties he was fine because there was little to get worked up about, but then when Vatican II came along, things began to unravel for him. He felt there were growing pressures in the Church which would lead to an explosion - and there he was both right and wrong - and he began to dig his heels in, deploring change of any kind and yearning for the old certainties. I could see the subtle change in him as he became resentful and bitter in a way that had certainly not been true before. That made him cling to time-hallowed practices like devotions and his daily Office, and the rest of parish activity began to feel threatening, as if he never knew into what strange territories it might lead him.'

'When you say he was both right and wrong about the effects of Vatican II, what do you mean? I ask because the inspector thinks that the seeds of your father's murder might lie in the council: he was killed for what he stood for, not for who he was as a person.'

'I see, that's interesting,' Fay said. 'Well, he took an interest in the council as it was proceeding. He would read the Catholic press and take note of what was coming out of Rome, but he felt that the council was breaking down barriers but not erecting anything in their place. He said it was like letting cattle out of a field to roam wild, and the result could only be a loss of focus, a loss of unity, a loss of direction, and I believe he was right. The trouble was that individuals went off on their own: if the Church had acted differently in the aftermath of the council, the results would not have been so dramatic. As it was, priests and laity began drifting off, and there was no one capable of bringing them back; and in any case no one knew what they would be coming back *for* - or *to*. Those who left were generally the brighter, more alert types, impatient that changes were being implemented either too slowly or not at all, while those who stayed behind continued, or tried to continue, as if the council had never been. I exaggerate, but probably not by much. So my father became rather disillusioned. He could see, in the latter two curates he had, the damage, as he saw it, being inflicted on young priests by the seminaries, and he deplored it.'

'Your father had another fear, I understand, Mr Fay, and I hope you won't mind my mentioning it: he feared his mental faculties were slipping.'

'He did, I'm afraid, and the saddest part of it is, I think it was true. That's why I was at his church last week. You see, he had not long had a session with a psycho-geriatrician, I think they call them, and the result was not encouraging. He was so cast down by this, as he had hoped to complete at least a further seven years of priestly ministry before offering to retire, that I got quite alarmed, and I offered to take him out for a meal. I arrived at the presbytery at half-six, forgetting that he was hearing confessions and giving Benediction, so I sat in the front row just to tell him I had arrived and would be waiting for him outside afterwards. He squeezed my hand and said he would join me as soon as he could. Those were the last words we exchanged.'

Spooner allowed a few minutes to elapse as he witnessed the man's grief. He changed the subject.

'What about your Aunt Maud, Mr Fay?'

'Oh, her! She thought I was nothing but a nuisance. I was a mistake to start with and hung round my father's neck like an albatross, preventing him from making the most of himself. But why blame me? I didn't ask to be born out of wedlock.'

'How did she and your father get on?'

'All right, I think. Maud is three years older than my father and is, to my way of thinking, a bit of a battleaxe. I think my father stood slightly in awe of her.'

'Was she like-minded in matters religious?'

'Yes, very much so. She couldn't stand all this English business at Mass, and she scorned young priests as feeble-minded and airy-fairy. If she were out to do murder, she would rather have gone for Fr Gabriel!'

On that lighter note, Spooner took his leave of the castle administrator and was glad to be told that they would meet again that evening.

While Spooner was thus engaged at Kenilworth, Wickfield was busy contacting those who would take part in the evening's event, and he needed in addition to the previous cast a stranger to act as a pretend killer. He did not think Fr Gabriel need attend, either in his own right or as a substitute for Fr Wilfred; he might indeed be nothing but a distraction. Wickfield intended to re-enact the events from the moment Fr Wilfred entered the sacristy from the presbytery at approximately five-and-twenty past six to the moment when the dead priest was laid on the sofa in his living-room. The role of Fr Wilfred was being taken by a policeman, but this man did not promise to fall out of the confessional into a heap on the floor exactly as the poor priest had done, and he asked his audience to be tolerant. The entire cast assembled at a quarter past six in the presbytery, to be briefed by Inspector Wickfield. The supposed murderer, a colleague from the police station, was, however, kept concealed from the other players.

'Right, Ladies and Gentlemen, may I say first of all how grateful we are to you for agreeing to take part in this reconstruction? We have a vague idea how the murder was committed, and possibly some idea as to motive, but none of that is to concern you. It is most important that you carry out your own movements exactly as you remember them, without regard for anything else that may be going on or for anybody else. You will have an opportunity at the close to make any comments that come to mind.'

'Inspector, what do I do if I can't remember exactly what I did?'

'Don't worry about it: do your best. Whatever you do, don't start asking questions!' This sally was greeted with appreciative titters.

'And what do I do,' asked another, 'if I make a mistake?'

'You'll have to carry on regardless; there's nothing else you can do.' After a second or two, he continued.

'Now Sergeant Spooner and I will be sitting or standing for the duration at the back of the church: please ignore us entirely. When you estimate that your time of arrival has come, move from where we are in the presbytery to outside and through the main door of the church, and then do exactly as you did last Thursday, as near as you can remember it. Move around, read, pray, light a candle, leave the church, just as you did, without regard for anyone else. The five of you who are going to confession must just pretend there is a priest there. The shutters may not move, as our replacement confessor may get confused' – polite laughter at this point - 'and you may be facing a blank piece of wood, but try to carry on as normal. You will have to do your best to estimate the length of time you spent in the confessional. If you left the church before the time of Benediction, simply make your way back into the presbytery and wait for the rest of us to join you at a little after seven. Then at the end, as I say, we shall ask you all for your comments.'

'Ooh, isn't this exciting!' There was no doubting whence this comment emanated. Wickfield ignored it and continued.

'You are all equally important, whether you think you saw anything relevant last Thursday or not. Those of you who carry the body into the presbytery may not remember the manoeuvre in every detail, but that may not matter. Just do your best. Mr Jennings has set the church lighting as it was, and he will remain in the sacristy until a few minutes after seven. You should find everything as it was that Thursday. Now, are there any further questions?'

He could feel a certain tension in his audience: they were nervous and rehearsing their parts in their heads, but there were no further questions.

'Right, let us begin.'

For Wickfield and Spooner at their vantage point at the back of the church, there was no means of judging how accurate the re-enactment was, but all they could say afterwards was that it *felt* right. The only sounds were of traffic on the road and the rustle of clothes as people moved about the church or shifted in their seats. Mr Fay sat at the front, and when his part was concluded, he got up and slowly left the church. The penitents came and went. As Mr Foynes came out of the confessional at a little after five minutes to seven, the unmentioned second policeman moved across the top of the church, where he had been lighting a candle to the Virgin Mary, walked slowly down the aisle on the 'epistle' side of the church, paused outside the confessional and made a small movement before making his exit. Mr Jennings appeared, the body tumbled (more or less) out of the confessional and was carried away. The re-enactment was over.

Wickfield had arranged for wine and a few canapés to be served in the presbytery, by way of thanks, oiling the interface between the police and the public, and, calling for silence – although there was little enough conversation after the grave events of the previous half-hour – he invited comments. Fr Gabriel had joined them, wrenching himself away, he explained, from preparing his sermon for the morrow.

'Tomorrow is what we call Septuagesima Sunday, Inspector, and the gospel is the parable of the Workers in the Vineyard, from chapter twenty of Matthew. I'm trying to work in something about Fr Wilfred – perhaps as one of the workers who had endured the heat of the day – but I'm not finding it easy to do the reading justice at the same time. I know we were given plenty of advice at Oscott on how to draw up a sermon, but it's a different matter when you're standing there in the flesh. I'm quite glad of a break, really!'

'Now,' the inspector said, 'are there any comments people would like to make?'

'Yes, Inspector,' said some woman, 'I don't remember that last man who walked down past the confessional. He was new, wasn't he?'

'Well, imagine he had walked down five or even ten minutes earlier. Would you have recognised him then?'

The woman could not be quite so sure, but a man piped up.

'No, I don't remember him either, Inspector. To me he stuck out.'

'How do folks feel the reconstruction went on the whole?' Wickfield asked. There was a general murmur to the effect that they had done pretty well, considering! 'Has anyone any ideas as to how the murder might have been committed?' No one ventured to accuse one of the penitents; so no, no one had any idea.

'Well, Ladies and Gentlemen, thank you so much for your time and patience. I hope this will help us clear up who murdered your parish priest and why.'

Seven

Wickfield summoned Spooner to his office first thing on Monday morning.

'I have a spot of news for you, Sergeant.'

'Yes, Sir, I hope it's good news.'

'Well, yes, I think one might say that: I've had an idea!'

'Good heavens! No, I didn't mean it that way, Sir!'

'No, no, I'm sure you didn't. I have been busy, and I think I know how the murder was done, who did it, and why.'

'Well, that's marvellous: congratulations! How did this miracle of insight come about, if I may ask?'

'Yes, you may ask, but your phrase "miracle of insight" smacks of disbelief and insubordination. No more of that, please,' he said with a huge smile. 'It so happens that I had a brainwave. During Saturday evening's reconstruction, two thoughts came to me. First of all, because the possibility of someone walking down the side aisle and stabbing Fr Wilfred through the door of the confessional did not seem to receive endorsement from those present, I thought around a bit more. Then yesterday I went over to Droitwich, firstly to put a question to Fr Gabriel, and secondly to examine the confessional more closely with my new idea in mind. I also took the opportunity to stay for Mass, to get a feel for the parish at worship.'

'And what question did you put to Fr Gabriel?'

'I told him I thought I had worked out the who, the why and the how of the murder, but I wasn't yet sure enough of my ground to make an arrest, and I certainly didn't wish to make any accusation at that stage. I then asked him simply whether it was thought or known that Thomas Foynes was gay.' Spooner looked bewildered.

'What relevance can that have on the matter?' he asked.

'Oh, lots. And my examination of the confessional was also very revealing.'

'Well, go on, Sir, don't keep me in suspense.'

At that moment one of Wickfield's colleagues knocked on the door and entered with a letter in his hand.

'Excuse my interrupting, Stan, but I thought you'd like to see this as soon as possible. It might just be interesting, you never know.'

It was a buff envelope, standard 9" x 6 ½", addressed to The Detective in charge of the Sacred Heart Murder Case and franked in Birmingham. Wickfield turned it over, handed it to Spooner for his inspection, retrieved it and then slit it open with a paper-knife. He drew out a thin booklet with, on its pale red cover, the curious title *Bloodletting in the Body Ecclesiastic*, printed crimson drops oozing down the page off the first word. The author was given as A Priest of the Birmingham Diocese, and it was, according to information at the foot of the page, privately printed in 1908. After the title page came a short table of contents:

I Schism
II Heresy
III The Papacy

and then a Foreword. Wickfield read as follows: he was riveted from the start.

Foreword

Let me state at the outset what this Booklet is not: it is *not* an attack on Holy Mother Church; it is *not* the work of an atheistical enemy of the Vatican; it is *not* an assault on Catholic history by a disenchanted priest. What is it, therefore? It is an attempt by a devout, dedicated and obedient member of the English clergy to express sorrow and regret for countless acts of violence perpetrated on perceived critics and foes by Those Who Should Know Better, namely people in power at the Church's heart.

It is also not a complete and scientifically researched paper on the subject of

Roman acts of injustice and aggression. The reader is referred to bigger and better works than this one. The present writer has one small purpose in mind: to draw its readers' attention to the use of violence as a way of dealing with awkward critics of the hierarchy and to state, firmly and loudly, that he deplores it with all the fibre of his being.

This short work is in three parts. The first two look at the way in which the Church has dealt with those labelled Schismatics and Heretics. The third part takes a slightly different approach, as will appear in its place. Critics internal and external have rarely been treated with courtesy and rational dialogue. They are much more likely to have met denunciation, insult, banishment and imprisonment, censorship, unfair trial, torture and death. This solitary priest in his presbytery would like to make amends in so far as his means and knowledge permit. *Deus eum adjuvet.*

[Pages 3-12 had been torn out, and the booklet continued and concluded with Part III.]

III <u>The Papacy</u>

In the first two parts of this booklet, we have given the Reader a brief account of some famous Schismatics and Heretics — or at least of some so called by those whose views eventually prevailed. In this Third Part we consider Popes Who Have Been Murdered. This calls for no little clarification. Between the years 882 and 1305, of eighty-seven Popes some fifteen are often considered to have been murdered. In the early centuries of the Church, many Popes lost their lives in persecutions, and many have been canonised, officially or not, as a consequence. We are not concerned with these holy men. For later periods — those under discussion - we are hampered in our exposition by absent or obscure historical data, and four comments are in order:

1. Of some Popes, not only is it difficult to identify a single *gestum* or *dictum* reliably; it is not even possible to identify such crucial data as dates of birth, of election (not always the appropriate word, since many were foisted on the Church or seized power themselves) and of death.

2. Names and titles are disputed. So, for example, depending on which source one consults, Pope Stephen, who is thought to have reigned from December 939 to February 942, a little over two years, is the VI, VII or VIII of that name.

3. There were numerous AntiPopes: Christopher, Boniface VII, John XVI, Gregory VI, Benedict X, Honorius II, Clement III (twice!) and at least eleven others, all claiming legitimacy by rights of election, appointment or war and all acknowledged as Pope by one or more factions in the Church and/or Empire.

4. Some Popes were murdered by their enemies, some by their friends. By that I mean that Popes were eliminated as rivals or obstacles on the one hand or, on the

other, purged as warts on the Body Ecclesiastic. It is not always easy to discern one from the other.

With these cautions, and wishing also to reiterate my admission that I am not an Historian of the period, I proceed to give a chronological account of the fifteen murdered Popes under discussion. I shall then, with suitable reservations, draw a modest but firm conclusion before proceeding to some slight theological considerations. (If the Reader wants Cajetan, he must go to Cajetan!)

1. John VIII (872-882) was a Roman who lived in troubled times and did his best(?) to counter threats from the Saracens, disturbances in the Eastern Church, political battles in Charlemagne's old Empire. An unreliable legend has him poisoned and then, when the poison was working too slowly, battered to death with a hammer by a relation of his who coveted his supposed wealth. The details of his death are obscure and probably, as I say, legendary, but it is generally accepted at the least that he was murdered.

2. (H)adrian III (884-885). Adrian also was Roman, but very little is known of his life or papacy. The prevailing consensus is that he was murdered by his enemies on his way to attend a Diet at Worms, his 'enemies' being members of an aristocratic faction opposed to his open support for an imperial candidate.

3. Stephen VI (or VII) (896-897). Stephen, often diagnosed by historians as mad, is particularly known for his star role in the so-called Cadaver Synod (the 'Synodus Horrenda' of the history books), held in the Basilica of St John Lateran to express his outrage at the reign of his predecessor but one, Pope Formosus (891-896), and immortalised in English in part of Robert Browning's *The Ring and the Book*. However, what concerns us here is his death. He was seemingly deposed, imprisoned and strangled on the orders of his successor, who honoured the memory of the dead Formosus.

4. Leo V (903). He reigned for thirty days before being strangled by Antipope Christopher or, in another version, by Pope Sergius III (whose illegitimate son was elected Pope as John XI in 931. It is astonishing that Pope Sergius III, one of the most violent and immoral men ever to have occupied the throne of St Peter, apparently died of natural causes after a quite shocking reign of seven years).

5. John X (914-928). He seems to have been an Italian, and he enjoyed an unusually long reign, mainly by allying himself with powerful secular interests. He was smothered in prison on his mistress's orders.

6. Stephen VII (or VI, VIII or even IX) (939-942). His biographical details are scant and uncertain, although many commentators think he was German. He was imprisoned by Alberic Prince of Rome and died in prison.

7. John XII (955-964), son of Prince Alberic and himself both Prince and Pope and leading light in the so-called *Saeculum obscurum*, arguably the papacy's lowest

moment. He has gone down in history as the only man to be elected Pope as a teenager. He seems to have been killed by a man whom he was cuckolding.

8. <u>Benedict VI</u> (973-974), who reigned for some eighteen months. His nationality and date of birth are unknown, but he may have been a Roman. When his protector, the Emperor, died, the citizens of Rome rose against him, and Crescentius, brother of his predecessor John XIII, gave orders for him to be strangled in Castel S.Angelo in Rome.

9. <u>John XIV</u> (983-984). He was from Pavia in Lombardy. Like Benedict VI, he died in Castel S.Angelo prison, either by starvation or by poison. This was on the orders of Antipope Boniface VII, who was created 'Pope' in 984 by the same Crescentius. Incidentally, Crescentius himself eventually met a very unpleasant death in the same castle, but that is not part of our story.

10. <u>Gregory V</u> (996-999), usually considered the first German Pope. He died suddenly at the early age of 27, having been made Pope at the age of 24, and it has often been suggested that he died as the result of foul play.

11. <u>Sergius IV</u> (1009-1012). He was a Roman. Since he died less than a week after his infamous patron Crescentius (see above), his death is often attributed to murder.

12. <u>Clement II</u> (1046-1047). Another German, he managed to reign for nine months only, before dying of poison. Enemies of the Church ascribe his death to a deliberate act of hostile elements within the Roman Curia, whereas other, less biased, historians, consider the death to be accidental. Pope Clement II is the only Pope buried north of the Alps: but that is a curiosity beyond our remit.

13. <u>Damasus II</u> (1048). He is the third German Pope, succeeding Clement II by virtue of the armies of Emperor Henry III but dying only three weeks after taking office. It is sometimes suggested that he was poisoned to death, but other accounts attribute his death to malaria. His age at death is unknown.

14. <u>Boniface VIII</u> (1294-1303). Boniface seemingly died of his injuries after a severe beating on the order of King Philip IV of France, with the cooperation of the Colonna family. His 'crime' was to wish to claim secular as well as spiritual power: kings were to be subordinate to the Church's authority.

15. <u>Benedict XI</u> (1303-1304). He was an Italian and reigned as Pope for eight months, dying at the age of 64. [Can anyone imagine the Carpenter of Nazareth 'reigning' in Israel?] He was allegedly poisoned by the same people who disposed of Boniface VIII and for roughly the same reason.

It is accepted by the present Author that the period 850-1050 was an unusual and uncharacteristic time in the history of the Catholic Church. The political and social

---

The sixty years between the election of Sergius III (904) and the death of John XII (964). The phrase is Baronius'. Pornocracy, another term for it often found in the literature, is a Protestant term of contempt.

circumstances of the time did not permit a settled and considered functioning of the Organs of Power in the Catholic Church. The death of Charlemagne opened up a time of unprecedented upheaval in Europe in which standards of civilisation — education, literature, the arts, social intercourse, courtly life and so on — fell to abysmal depths. For many years, particularly later on in the period under consideration in the present Booklet, Rome was ruled — misruled, one should rather say — by squabbling baronial families vying with each other for power from bases in their fortresses and determined to lay hands on the plum of authority, the Roman See. Battles swayed to and fro as now one family, now another — the Sanguignas, the Counts of Tusculum, the Savellis, the Orsinis, the Caetanis, the Colonnas — gained the ascendancy. Popes were often puppets of secular forces, powerless to impose gospel values on a corrupt and lawless world, even if they had wished to. Others, however, were leading actors in the internecine struggles, proud to have achieved power and anxious to hold on to it.

No Catholic can be proud of this record, despite making all allowances for the manipulative and violent methods of non-Church factions which battered the Church into submission. The Church — by which I mean the Official Church, the officers elected by their peers or appointed by their superiors to provide guidance and leadership to their flock - had so allied itself with secular authority that the two were often indistinguishable, and diabolical values were allowed to gain the upper hand. Who is to blame? The Official Church! My reason for this outrageous claim is as follows.

In the preceding centuries, the Popes and cardinals and bishops had slipped gradually into regarding power as a reward and a privilege, not as a service. They had built castles, palaces and imposing mansions, cultivated the patronage of the powerful and wealthy, demanded tribute from the faithful to maintain their power-bases, extended their influence over every aspect of mediaeval life, elevated themselves into a clerical caste which brooked no criticism or opposition, arrogated titles to themselves specifically forbidden in the Gospels: in a word, they had lorded it over the Christian faithful. Some historians maintain that the decadence began in Constantine's time with a long series of Roman Popes, starting with Pope Sylvester I (314-335) and culminating in Pope Gregory I (590-604), but I am not qualified to judge this assessment. The slide was gradual and probably imperceptible, BUT, in a Church who claimed a Divine Founder and the constant assistance of the Holy Ghost, INEXCUSABLE! It is not my intention to shock the Reader with capital letters, but I must give vent to my feelings! The supposed pastors had transformed the House of God from a place of prayer into a Den of Thieves.

Worthy Popes have been murdered by ambitious and wicked men (and women), but ambitious and wicked Popes have also been murdered by those who perhaps — who at this distance of time can judge? — intended to restore some semblance of decency and order to the Church. Given the scant nature of the historical record, firm and wide-ranging conclusions in the context of the present Work are not possible, but a provisional and tentative conclusion, which I put forward with all respect and humility, is that if the Church uses violence to suppress dissent — if she teaches by her actions that violence is a legitimate and appropriate means to solve problems of public order and opposition, of schism and heresy — she must not be surprised when individuals take it on themselves to remove unworthy Popes.

I wish now to turn to the teachings of St Thomas Aquinas to add theological weight to these remarks. St Thomas' main statement on the matter, imperfect though it is, occurs at *Summa theologiae* II-II, q.42, a.2, ad 3. Now I am no scholar, but I reckon I can read St Thomas and enjoy him! The passage says (in my own translation):

A tyrannical regime is unjust because its aim is not the common good but the tyrant's private good, as Aristotle makes clear. The disruption of such a regime is therefore not sedition [which is forbidden in Thomas' moral theology], except perhaps when the tyrannical regime is disrupted inordinately. In this latter case, the subject multitude suffers greater harm from the consequent upheavals than from the tyrannical regime itself. The worst tyrant of all is one who foments discord and sedition in the population over which he rules in order to dominate them in greater safety. Such sedition is tyrannical because it is ordained to the ruler's own good, with much harm to the multitude.

We need to add to this a short passage from a few pages further on (II-II, q.64, a.2, *in corpore*):

And so if anyone is a danger to the community and a corruptive influence because of anything sinful, it is praiseworthy and healthy [*laudabilis et salubris*] to kill him so that the common good can be preserved.

(There are other passages which in a complete and systematic treatment of the subject would add further principles and necessary nuances.) Thomas seems to have thought that the removal of a tyrant is legitimate for the sake of good order in the community but that the individual is not entitled to arrogate such a work to himself. It is the task (not exactly a duty) of the *public body*. An individual has such a right only if he can be certain of enjoying the support of the majority and so becoming as it were the spokesman of the many.

I should like to add one further authority: Joseph Mayol, who was the Dominican Provincial of Toulouse province in the last years of the seventeenth century and who published his *Summa moralis doctrinae Thomisticae circa decem praecepta Decalogi. Item virtutum Theologicarum Fidei, Spei & Charitatis, vitiaque illis opposita : nec non circa propositiones morales de hac materia ab Ecclesia damnatas, variis in locis sparsas* at Avignon in 1704. (Caveat: this immensely long volume — 800 quarto pages — is not for the timid!). In discussing the fifth of the Ten Commandments ('Thou shalt not kill'), he begins by asking the related questions: 'May public authorities put sinners to death?' and 'May private individuals kill wrongdoers?' (q.1, art.1 and 2). Mayol's answers, in a nutshell, are, to the first question, Yes, they may and must; to the second, No, they may not, except in two specific cases: self-defence and on God's specific orders, or, in Thomas' own words quoted by Mayol, *zelo Dei commotus*: moved by zeal for God. (The specific case under consideration is Phinehas' assassination of an Israelite man and a Midianite woman by pinning them together with a spear, in Numbers chap. 25.) My impression of Mayol's text is that the Author grants permission grudgingly, as a last resort in circumstances of extreme necessity.

And so to my conclusions. The Reader who has followed me thus far will agree, I trust, with the following formulation:

> Despite defences offered by some theological authorities, violence, whether verbal or physical, has no place whatever in the conduct of Church affairs (Parts I and II); contrariwise, moderate violence, even to death, may be required, for the sake of the health of the whole Body Ecclesiastic, if power is usurped by a sinner (Part III).

Let Scripture have the final word:

In carne enim ambulantes non secundum carnem militamus. For though we walk in the flesh, we do not wage war according to the flesh (II Cor.x.3).

He passed the booklet over to the sergeant, and then sat there, ruminating, while his junior absorbed the contents, with – judging from his immobility and furrowed forehead – a concentration and absorption equal to his own.

'Well,' Wickfield exclaimed. 'How very interesting!'

'But what does it all mean? Who sent this, and why?'

'When I was talking to Miss Warren after Thursday's choir-session, she said something like, "If even popes can get themselves murdered, why not parish priests?" Now this booklet – well, not the booklet itself, but the sending of it – is either a confession or a tip-off. That's how I read it, anyway. It's either someone saying, "Look, I murdered poor old Fr Wilfred, but I did it for the good of the parish," or it's someone telling us, "Look out for someone who thinks he or she is doing the parish a favour by disposing of a sinful priest". I think that in the first instance you and I need to have a further word with Miss Warren.'

'But you were about to tell me, before that booklet arrived, about your new theory. Can't I hear it?'

'You can, you certainly can, and funnily enough, it involves our Miss Warren and fits in perfectly with this booklet. It goes like this. As I was saying, Saturday's reconstruction suggested to us that the idea of a killer committing the murder through the doors of the confessional received no backing. The key had therefore to be in the wings of the confessional; it *had* to be. Yesterday, therefore, with Fr Gabriel's acquiescence, I had an even closer examination of the box, and I found, to my gratification, that the grille at the altar end had been tampered with. Its seating has been altered so that the grille can now be lifted out and replaced with the minimum of fuss, whereas the other one is still fixed fast. I spotted it because there is the thinnest imaginable white line of original wood where the varnish on the frame and the varnish on the grille no longer quite meet. I returned to a previous idea of ours, therefore, a conspiracy, and with this in mind went over the penitents again. Let me remind of their order of appearance, as it were: Mrs Green, Mr Ross, Miss Bradford, Miss Warren and Mr Foynes. The three who used the altar-end of the confessional were Mrs Green, Miss Bradford and Miss Warren. Now the murder had to be committed by someone at the altar-end, where the dodgy grille is. If Mrs Green is the killer, all other four penitents were in the know and played the game. Doubtful – at this stage of our knowledge, anyway. What about Miss Bradford, then? Just too dizzy, in my opinion, and in any case she could never be relied on to keep her mouth shut afterwards. I hope I'm not doing the young lady an injustice, because underneath it all, she strikes me as being a very pleasant and serious-minded person. That leaves Miss Warren. She *has* to be the killer: elderly, erudite spinster Tabitha Warren. There's just nobody else. If she's the killer, however, our Mr Foynes is in it too, because he told us he went to confession and spoke with Fr Wilfred. I asked myself what could the connection be between these last two penitents. At the moment I have only a theory, and it's this – between ourselves, of course. Foynes is a devout, even intense, Catholic, and aspires to the Catholic priesthood. He applies to the archdiocese, and they, as usual, request a character reference from his parish priest. Fr Tarbuck feels unable to endorse his parishioner's aspirations, because of his sexuality, and therefore replies to the authorities, I'm sorry, a lovely man, really holy and well-meaning, but it's no go, he's gay. When Foynes is duly turned down, he is furious – and depressed – and vows vengeance. He confides in Miss Warren, perhaps because she's an aunt, or a past teacher or something, and she comes up with this little scheme. She too regards Fr Tarbuck as an obstacle to effective Catholicism and is happy to join with Foynes in a spot of murder. How's that?'

'It's brilliant, Sir, but how are we going to prove it?'

'Ah, I don't know, but the first step is to interview Miss Warren and then Mr Foynes – again.'

Eight

Wickfield had not yet moved from his chair in order to execute his latest purpose when his telephone rang. It was the housekeeper at the Sacred Heart Church, Droitwich.

'It's Pat Gould, Inspector, from the Sacred Heart.'

'Yes, Mrs Gould, what can I do for you?'

'I'm so worried: Fr Gabriel's gone missing!'

'What?' Wickfield jerked himself upright in the extremity of his surprise. 'How do you know? I mean, couldn't he have just gone off to see friends?'

'Oh, no, Inspector. You see, for a start, his bed wasn't slept in last night. Then this morning he never turned up for Mass at eight o'clock.'

'But it's a bit early to be talking about going missing, isn't it? There must be a perfectly rational explanation.'

'Well, I can't think of one, Inspector. Fr Gabriel would never have gone off like that without letting me know. I wish you'd come over.'

Wickfield and Spooner found themselves yet again making the journey out to Droitwich. They found a worried Mrs Gould half-heartedly waving a duster round the presbytery.

'I'm so glad you've come, Gentlemen, I'm that vexed.'

'First of all, Mrs Gould, just outline what happened this morning, if you would.'

'Well, Inspector, most days I come in at about half-past eleven to get some lunch for the two priests, but on a Monday I come in at nine o'clock and do the housework downstairs. On a Thursday I do the housework upstairs. I found the church locked, whereas Fr Gabriel should have said Mass at eight, and then, when I went into the presbytery, the place was empty. He hadn't had any breakfast, not that I could see; he hadn't even made himself a cup of tea. So I went upstairs, and his bed hadn't been slept in. I looked for some sort of note, but there was nothing. That's when I decided to phone you.'

'Well, we know he was here yesterday morning for Mass, because I spoke to him myself. What commitments at the church might he have on a Sunday afternoon?'

'Oh, none. Of course, there could always be a call for a visit, but normally nothing happens until Youth Club at eight, and even then the priests didn't feel *obliged* to attend because Gavin Healy is in charge and does a very good job of it.'

'Did Fr Gabriel have lunch at the presbytery yesterday?'

'Oh, yes, and the priest from Oscott, I forget his name. I always give them a roast on Sunday, and they were both here.'

'Have you checked whether his car is still here? Where does he keep it?'

'Oh, he's got no car: he goes around on a bicycle, although I've heard him mention the possibility of getting a small scooter. But he could easily have caught a bus or a train.'

'Right, Mrs Gould, leave it with us. We'll make a few inquiries. Do you know where his family come from?'

'Not exactly. Birmingham some way, but I'm not sure where.'

'Close friends?'

'The only one I know of is young Fr Sheridan, curate at Our Lady of the Rosary at Saltley. They often meet on their days off.'

'Good. Well, you get on, and we'll get busy.'

Wickfield and Spooner returned to Worcester to make their inquiries, but on the way the latter said to the former,

'You know, Sir, I'm not sure I like this very much. If Fr Gabriel's gone awol, that can only mean one of two things: either he's guilty and has got the wind up, because he thought, after your conversation yesterday, that you were getting on to him; or he's been abducted and possibly murdered.'

'That's a bit dramatic, isn't it, Sergeant? He could have gone off for any number of reasons: we just haven't got enough information yet.'

'No, we haven't, but where was he on the night his parish priest was murdered? We haven't discovered that. I don't see how he could have had anything to do with Fr Wilfred's death, but you never know.'

At Worcester Police Station, Inspector Wickfield telephoned the diocesan offices at the cathedral and asked to be put through to the vicar-general, Mgr Vincent Bagnall. (Wickfield thought that he would never master all the honorifics: the monsignors, the lordships, the graces, the eminences, the reverends and very reverends and right reverends and most reverends: what were they all *for*, apart presumably from the gratification and aggrandisement of the recipients?) He explained, in a quiet voice, what seemed to have happened, and his information was met with dismay.

'What can we do, Inspector? This is very serious indeed, unless it's just a blip.'

'Well, if you have any leads, please follow them up, but we are going to contact his family first and then Fr – Sheridan, is it? - at Saltley. Could you give me the address of Fr Gabriel's parents, and I'll pay them a visit? At the moment, we are just hoping he has hidden himself away rather than come to harm.' He omitted to add that the priest's unexpected absence had raised a probably quite groundless suspicion in their minds.

So it was that Wickfield and Spooner found themselves journeying, on a clear but cold Monday in late February, to Woodbrooke Road in Bournville, one of Birmingham's southern suburbs. The twenty-mile journey had occupied an unconscionable amount of time, what with road-works, traffic-lights, roundabouts, thoughtless pedestrians wishing to cross the road at belisha beacons and a seemingly inordinate amount of traffic. They arrived in the early afternoon and parked in what they found to be, in common parlance, a leafy suburb. The street comprised semi-detached houses and detached houses and was lined with linden trees. Mrs Winterton was doing the family ironing; her husband was at work. Their son Gabriel was not at home – but why should he be? – and no, he had not contacted them in the last twenty-four hours. Did she have any idea where he might be? Look, what was all this about? When the matter was clarified, Mrs Winterton, beginning to look rather concerned, suggested first Saltley, then the priest's siblings. Before moving on to Saltley, however, Wickfield asked Mrs Winterton whether she could think of any reason why her son might have temporarily disappeared.

'I think the strain of recent events has all been too much for him, Inspector,' she said. 'I mean, there he is, in charge of a parish, with no permanent help, and his parish priest hardly cold in his grave after a brutal murder. No wonder he's taken a bit of time out!'

'I'm sure you're right, Mrs Winterton, but we do need to find him. When did you last see him, may I ask?'

'Ooh, probably the week before last, but he phoned one day last week to tell us how the whole business was getting him down.'

'Yes, I can understand that. He strikes me as being a very serious priest who wouldn't abandon his post without good reason.'

'Oh, yes, he's serious all right. He wanted to be a priest from the age of thirteen or fourteen; nothing else would do, so after school he went off to Oscott for six years and loved it.'

'Did the prospect of a lifetime's celibacy not daunt him at that young age?'

'It might have done, but he never discussed it with us – or perhaps I should say with me. My husband may know differently.'

'Did he have girlfriends at school?'

'No, not that I know of. He was all for the priesthood.'

'And how has he found the reality of priesthood, do you know?'

'Well, I think he has found his first year and a half difficult. Fr Tarbuck was not an easy man to get on with – at least, so he tells me – and personally he found the parish rather run down. No, that's perhaps the wrong word: stagnant, marking time, not going anywhere, that might be better. He was keen to galvanise the people, but Fr Tarbuck was reluctant to support him.'

'Does Gabriel ever contemplate innovation without the parish priest's permission?'

'No, I wouldn't think so. Well, he couldn't anyway: he's tightly controlled.'

'That puts demands on his sense of obedience.'

'It does, and I think that's why he's not been entirely happy. He sees the good that could be done, he admires the laity for their enthusiasm and ideas, but all he meets is system and tradition and the pre-conciliar Church: he can't seem to get anywhere.'

'Ah,' said Wickfield, 'I wondered how long it would be before we got to the council! It seems to be cropping up all over the place in this business.'

'It's been crucial to Catholic life these past five or six years. I know Gabriel was all for it.'

'We think that possibly the division in the parish between, for want of better words, the traditionalists and the progressives, might just possibly have a bearing on the murder. Might Gabriel know who was behind it, because if he does, he hasn't said anything about it to us.'

'That I wouldn't have an inkling about, I'm afraid, Inspector. I can tell you this, though: he would never himself have raised his hand in violence to further his hopes for the parish. Oh, no, not in a million years! And he would never have been party to such a scheme, either.'

'May I just ask what your husband does for a living?'

'He's a consultant dermatologist at Moseley Hall Hospital in the city.'

'And are you both Catholics?'

'No, I'm not, but my husband is very committed. He was delighted when our last son told us he wanted to become a priest.'

Gabriel Winterton had two brothers, Simon and Harrison, both older, both married and both in the Midlands. He asked Mrs Winterton whether she would mind telephoning them, either at home or at work, but there was no news in those quarters. He asked her to add on his behalf that if they heard anything, they were to contact the authorities immediately. There being no more seemingly to be done at Bournville, the inspector and his sergeant moved on to Saltley.

Saltley, an inner-city suburb of Birmingham, offered a very different aspect to the visitors. Here the housing was largely terraced, and it was apparent that immigrants were moving in in large numbers. The brick church of Our Lady of the Rosary was, to Wickfield's eye, rather functional than beautiful, and he thought it disappointing that beauty should seem to feature so low on architects' agendas. It was all a question of finance, he hazarded. The light was already fading in the late afternoon, with a sky that was now overcast and drizzle in the air, and Wickfield found himself hoping that his visit to Saltley would defy the weather and the surroundings and help lift his spirits. His ring at the bell was answered by a young man whom they took to be Fr Sheridan himself, casually but still smartly dressed, a mop of curly blonde hair surmounting an open face. He was friendly: he had no reason not to be. When Spooner had stated their business, the priest hesitated – dithered – and then yielded.

'You'd better come in,' he said. 'I suppose it was only a matter of time.'

Fr Gabriel, who was sitting in the living-room in an open-necked shirt and a woolly jumper, remembered etiquette sufficiently to the extent of standing and greeting the visitors, but it was clear that he was a troubled man. He looked as if he had slept and eaten little, forgotten to shave and forgotten his prayers: a tormented, haunted priest.

'You've led us a bit of dance, Father,' Wickfield said. 'It's taken us quite some time to catch up with you, and you've left a number of people rather worried. Before we begin any conversation, could I ask you, Fr Sheridan, to phone the vicar-general, Mrs Gould at Droitwich presbytery and Fr Gabriel's mother, just to let them know that we've arrived?'

When the resident priest disappeared to make the relevant telephone-calls, Fr Gabriel, to the detectives' deep embarrassment, began to sob in a heap on the sofa.

'So you've found me, Inspector! Yes, I killed Fr Wilfred. How am I ever going to live with myself?'

He raised a tear-stained face in which misery and self-reproach were branded. To his credit, Wickfield commented firmly,

'Nonsense, Father. You didn't kill him. We think we know who did, and it wasn't you!'

'It was,' Gabriel said with another sob. 'I as good as killed him.'

'That is nonsense, and deep within you, you know it. You and I need to have a chat, and you'll discover that you have nothing to reproach yourself for. Can I ask you to dry your eyes, have a bite to eat and become yourself again? This just won't do, you know.'

Fr Sheridan reappeared.

'Can you knock up a sandwich and a cup of coffee for our friend,' Wickfield said, 'and a cup of tea for us to keep him company wouldn't come amiss!'

Ten minutes later, order had been restored, and Wickfield offered no objection when Gabriel asked whether Matt could stay.

'Now look here, Fr Gabriel, we understand that the events of the last ten days have been demoralising for you, but you mustn't blame yourself. I know what you're thinking. You're thinking that you undermined Fr Wilfred and led someone in the parish to remove him as an obstacle to a renewal of Catholic life. Am I right?'

'Yes, Inspector, more or less. I left Oscott full of enthusiasm. I was going to apply the council's insights, and parish life would take off! We were going to look to cooperate with our fellow-Christians, we were going to create schemes in which we could work with our Muslim and Hindu neighbours, we were going to empower the laity, we were going to be a Church of the poor, and so forth. After eighteen months I had achieved nothing! All I had succeeded in doing was sowing dissent and unease. I split the parish. I made Fr Wilfred look like a fossil, and someone stepped in to finish him off.'

'Well, if it makes you feel better, there are several things I can say to that. The first is that you have made a huge difference to the parish, in only eighteen months. You have inspired people and offered leadership, not least in the way of obedience and piety. Secondly, I need to tell you two things you *probably* don't know; one of them you *certainly* don't know. The first is this, and' - looking at Fr Sheridan - 'I must ask that this goes absolutely no further for the moment, when he was eighteen, Fr Wilfred fathered a son. Now he was not yet in holy orders of any kind; he hadn't even applied to enter the seminary, but someone may have regarded him as unsuitable material for the priesthood. I'm right, aren't I: that's news to you?'

'Yes, completely! I had no idea.'

'Well, that brings me to my second point, which is certain to be news to you as well: at least, I hope it is! This morning, we received through the post, anonymously, part of a booklet written by a priest of the archdiocese sixty years ago.' Here Wickfield produced the copy. 'I want you to spend a few minutes reading it, if you would, and you can pass it on to Fr Matt.'

The minutes ticked by, and at the end of his reading of it, Fr Gabriel looked up inquiringly.

'What's it all about?'

'I can't tell you that as an expert: I'm not in the least qualified to judge the subject matter, but I think I can guess why it was sent to us. You see, the burden of this last part of the work is that sometimes, when power is usurped by a sinful and unsuitable person, the individual Christian, acting not on his own initiative but with the knowledge and consent of a wider constituency, has a duty to remove the usurper. As I say, I've no idea whether that accords with Scripture, or with the teachings of the Church, I'm only going by what I read here. Now someone, knowing about Fr Wilfred's past, has taken it into his or her head that he shouldn't have been ordained priest, or appointed as parish priest, or sent to Droitwich, I don't know which of those things annoys him most.'

Here Wickfield paused, uncertain whether to continue on to his next suggestion. He decided that he should.

'Or there is another possibility, and again I must ask you to keep this entirely to yourselves. A parishioner of yours may have been blocked from going forward for the priesthood because of his homosexuality, and certain parties may have blamed Fr Wilfred for this. It's but a short step from that to seeing Fr Wilfred as some sort of retrogressive block to progress in general, and some people take these things very seriously. So you see,' he concluded, 'you personally had nothing to do with his death. It is other people who have skewed the present situation to suit their own ends. No normal parishioner is going to think that killing a person for having a brief liaison at the age of eighteen makes any sort of sense.'

'Yes, I understand what you're saying,' Fr Gabriel said.

'You will have gathered that we still haven't exactly solved the crime, but we're working on a number of ideas, and none of them casts you as the murderer, and I put it to you that your going awol doesn't help the parish, or your superiors, or your family.'

Gabriel looked a little sheepish.

'I know,' he said, 'but I have been very discouraged over the past few months, and Fr Wilfred's murder was just the last straw.'

'You're lucky to have good friends in the business, but will you please tell me first next time you feel like doing a runner!'

'You know, Sergeant,' Wickfield said to his colleague as they found their car, 'why don't we pay a visit to Oscott while we're so close? We might find out something about this little booklet.' Travelling therefore through Gravelly Hill and Erdington, they found the college by dint of asking numerous people, and at a little after seven they drove through the gatehouse and up the curved drive to alight at the front terrace. Beyond the spacious grounds shrouded in darkness, they could see the lights of Birmingham stretching into the distance. At one time, they supposed, a century ago, the college would have been in open countryside, remote from the clamour of modern living, whereas now the city hustled its every boundary. Their ring at the bell was answered promptly, and they were shown into a small waiting room near the imposing orielled entrance-tower. In a few minutes the rector appeared, sombrely dressed in a black cassock, and when they had explained their business, he promised to send them the lecturer in Church history who would doubtless be able to assist them further.

'Would you be able to hang on a few minutes, Gentlemen? We're just finishing supper. He won't keep you long.'

The Church historian, Fr Henry Bancks, was a tall, spare man in his fifties, his face shadowed by bushy eyebrows and marked by a scar under his left eye. He walked with something of a limp. After mutual greetings in a suitably formal style, the priest said that he would be glad to help if he could: what exactly was the booklet about? After reading it through quickly, he said,

'The contents stretch into dogma and into moral theology, so I may not be your best man. What exactly is it you wished to know?'

'Fr Bancks, I should perhaps have told you beforehand, except that I wanted you to read the extract without preconceptions, that we are working on the murder of Fr Tarbuck at Droitwich.'

'Ah,' he said, 'yes, a terrible affair.'

'We were sent this anonymously this morning, and it presumably has some sort of bearing on the case, at least according to the envelope. Can I ask you first of all whether you knew of the existence of this booklet?'

'No, I don't think so. I don't think I've ever come across it, although of course there may be a copy in the library. We have a huge library, you know.'

'So you can't tell us who wrote it?'

'No, no idea, I'm sorry, but it probably doesn't matter, does it?'

'No, I shouldn't think so.'

'How good is it, as theology?'

'Well, that's a tricky question. Let me say this. It's a point of view – a valid point of view – but whether it's supported by the evidence adduced, I'm less certain. The trouble is that the writer is trying to squeeze very extensive and subtle arguments into the space of a few pages. For example, some of the popes mentioned *may* have been murdered, or, contrariwise, they may have died quietly in their beds, but if there's serious doubt, the writer really has no business mentioning them as part of his argument. In other words, he hasn't rigorously weighed and sifted through his material. Again, the arguments from Thomas Aquinas and Mayol are really only adumbrations. I mean, I'm not a dogmatic theologian, but my reaction to the pamphlet is that a lot more needs to be said on these points than the writer has put forward. You can't just quote a slice of Aquinas out of context and say, Well, that's it, then, folks, this is what Thomas thought on the subject. There are other relevant passages that he mentions, but I should look for a much more thorough discussion of *all* the texts. Theology is regarded by its practitioners as a science, using reasoned argument to advance from first principles to secondary conclusions, but traditionally the appeal to authority has been regarded as a clincher. The author of this pamphlet chooses two authorities who propound his point of view either partially or hesitantly; rather poor theology, I should have said.'

'So it's nonsense?'

'Oh, no, as I say, the writer has a valid point of view, and a book instead of a pamphlet may have borne out his argument, but as it stands, it's all a bit flimsy. There have been bad popes, no doubt about it. Influential families did force their candidates on to the Holy

See, and some individuals may have thought it their duty to exercise judicious, or even wholesale, pruning, but I'm not sure that is the basis for a considered argument in a pamphlet of thirty pages.'

'Well, to be fair to the author, he does acknowledge the booklet's limitations,' Wickfield said.

'He does, he does, that's certainly a saving grace.'

'If your library has a copy, would you be able find it, do you think, Father?'

'Yes, I should think so. Would you like to come with me, Gentlemen?'

The three men wound their way round the cloister floored in terrazzo and entered a heavy and studded oak door into a high room, galleried, full of books from floor to ceiling: an impressive sight. One or two students were dotted about under reading lamps. The priest took them to the index filed in metal cabinets and searched, presumably under Anon. His efforts were rewarded, and he went off, to return shortly with the complete work, in next to mint condition. Unfortunately the author was not named, and the work told them nothing of which they were unaware beforehand.

'I'm sorry we daren't let this out of the college,' Fr Bancks said apologetically. 'The librarian would have a fit!'

'No, no, that's quite all right. Reading the whole thing wouldn't help us anyway, I don't think. Any idea how many of these were printed?'

'No, and I'm not sure how you could find out if the figure isn't given in the booklet.'

'Could one get hold of one today?'

'Possibly, but I really can't help you there. I'm sorry to be so badly informed.'

Wickfield and Spooner took their leave, no wiser but glad to have seen the inside – and, if it comes to that, the outside – of the seminary for the first time in their lives.

Nine

*T*he following morning, not quite at first light but as early as they considered decent, Wickfield and Spooner called on Miss Warren, who occupied a terraced house not far from the church, in Oakland Avenue. Oakland Avenue is a quiet street, apart from a burst of commuter traffic morning and evening, and belongs to quiet people whose suburban, settled lives are the envy of less privileged citizens. Miss Warren, a long retired teacher of shorthand at a secretarial college in London, had returned to her origins in Droitwich to enjoy her declining years, wishing to know better her brother's two children and many grandchildren and the friends of her youth. She was tall, thin and angular, with a few hairs on her chin and wisps permanently in her face from an unruly white shock on her head. A slight stoop and an uncertain gait betrayed her years, but her confident speech and bright eye spoke of inner youth and animation. She showed no surprise at seeing the detectives, unannounced, so early on a Tuesday morning – her morning for a weekly cup of tea with a neighbour – and invited them in with every appearance of welcome.

'I hope this visit means that you're busy solving the case, Gentlemen,' she said. 'If you're on the spot and active, something at least is happening!'

'Well,' the inspector said diffidently, 'I wouldn't say the case is solved yet, not exactly. That's why we're here, Miss Warren: we think you can give us a bit of help.'

'I doubt that very much, Inspector, but it's nice of you to have such confidence. My ideas are only ideas, you know. Now sit down the pair of you, and I'll have a cup of tea ready in a jiffy.'

'No, thank you, Miss Warren,' Wickfield said uncharacteristically, and on behalf of both of them, 'we've not long had breakfast.'

'Very well, Inspector, you know best, I daresay. Now what can I do for you?'

The men had sat in arm chairs by the window, and Miss Warren now lapsed into a Queen Anne (or at least Queen Anne-style) walnut chair nearer the hearth. She looked at them expectantly. Wickfield produced the *Bloodletting* booklet.

'Have you ever seen this before, Miss Warren?' he asked, handing it over to his hostess.

'Good heavens, Inspector, so you've got one too! How enterprising of you! But wait a minute, you've cut half the pages out of yours. Mine's in perfect condition.' She rose unsteadily and hobbled over to an enormous bookshelf, whence, after a short search, she plucked a copy of the booklet from amongst a pile of pamphlets and waved it at them. She resumed her seat, holding it in her hand. This short jaunt across the room on Miss Warren's part had given Wickfield and Spooner time to recover their self-possession, after a momentary sense of shock and disbelief that had robbed both of them of the power of speech.

'Perhaps you'd be good enough to tell us what you know about it.'

'I know a lot about it,' said Miss Warren, 'but I can't imagine how it comes into your investigation. Do enlighten me,' she added playfully. Seeing no reason not to enlighten her, Wickfield nodded in his sergeant's direction, and he, responding to the cue almost like the fall guy to the straight man, said innocently,

'A copy of this booklet was sent to the police station yesterday, Miss Warren. It was addressed to the Detective in charge of the Sacred Heart Murder Case. We're wondering why.'

'Oh, I know nothing about that,' Miss Warren said, 'but I can tell you about the booklet. My uncle wrote it, you see, and he gave me a copy inscribed To My Favourite Niece.' She tipped it forward, so that they could see a handwritten dedication. 'I wasn't his favourite niece at all, but it was nice of him to say so, wasn't it? I appreciated it.'

Speech again deserted her two visitors. The revelation, made so artlessly, had taken them utterly by surprise.

'Please tell us more, Miss Warren,' the inspector managed to say.

'Yes, of course, it will be a pleasure. We older folk get a lot of enjoyment about reliving our past, you know. The past doesn't bounce about and surprise you. Let me tell you about my uncle, then. My mother was one of three children, all born in Droitwich in the 1860s, but when their father died young, the family were rather reduced financially. However, I needn't go into all that, need I? But do let me just say this. Did I tell you I was reading d'Azeglio?'

The men nodded.

'Yes, I think I did. Well, when the young Massimo decides to go to Rome to try his fortune as an artist, his mother – and, I may add, his brother, two servants and a four-horse carriage – goes with him, even though she was in poor health, and he comments – I can't remember the exact words, but it's near enough - "Nobody in the world suffered with such courage as she did", and I've often thought of my own mother that way. Anyway, my mother's elder brother, Frank, left school as soon as he could and got a job, to help out with the money, and then my mother's aunt died and left her a bit, so that one way or another the family survived. At first, you see, it was thought that my uncle Brian would have to get a job smartly too, but in the end it was agreed that he could go on to the priesthood. No money in it, you know, but then money wasn't such an urgent need in the family by then. So off to Oscott he went, and he was ordained priest – oh, dear, when would it have been? – well, about 1890, I should think. That was the year in which I was born, so nothing of what I've told you so far came to me as personal knowledge, you understand. I mean, it's what I've always understood about the family's history. History: such a solemn word, and according to – was it Voltaire? - "little else but a picture of human crimes and misfortunes", if I've got that right, when all it was in our case was a modest Catholic family growing up in a small town in the middle of the last century and never destined to make news. Well, uncle Brian was posted first to a curacy somewhere in the Black Country, I think, then on to a leafy parish in Oxfordshire – you could easily get the details from the archdiocesan records at St Chad's, I'm sure, Gentlemen, if you really wished to, but I don't think the details matter. At least, they don't to me. Then in 1907 he was appointed to his first post as parish priest. It was only a small parish – Nechells – but it was close enough to Oscott for him to be able to use the library on his days off, and he thought he would get his brain back into gear by attempting one or two short works. He used to walk it, you know; but that's by the bye. Over the next few years he produced a number of booklets. I don't know whether he ever tried to get them formally published. I don't think he did, but for him the important thing was to aim at a project, see it through and have something to show for it. Most of the works were based on historical subjects which gave opportunity for reflection and wider speculation. He did one on the Albigensian crusade and tied it in with Pius X's condemnations of modernism – a particularly good one, that, I thought: he called it "Carnage: by the Vatican" - and another was called, "The Jews and the Inquisition: the Abiding Scandal of Christian Antisemitism", and so on. I have them all, if you're interested, Gentlemen.'

The inspector and his sergeant demurred.

'How many did he write, Miss Warren?' Wickfield asked.

'Seven, one for each year he was at Nechells.'

'Didn't he ever get into trouble with the authorities?'

'Well, he did and he didn't. He printed off only a few dozen copies of each one, and they always included a statement to the effect that he was a loyal son of the Church – which he was. I think the archbishop, Edward Ilsley in those days – of course, he was only bishop to start with, because Birmingham was only a diocese – thought he would do more harm than good by gagging him, so he let him be, and he was right that the pamphlets created little stir, and in any case, when my uncle was moved to a bigger parish further from Birmingham and Oscott, his literary efforts ceased. That's about all I can tell you, Gentlemen.'

'And when did he die?'

'Um, 1950 or thereabouts.'

'Now, Miss Warren, have you any idea how somebody might get hold of a copy?'

'Not the faintest, Inspector.'

'What did your uncle do with his small print-run? Did he distribute them to friends?'

'Yes, that's about the size of it. He didn't want fame, much less fortune, so he just gave them away to anyone who wanted one. Half-a-dozen went to the family, the rest to priest friends. You see, Inspector, there's no mystery about it, as you seemed to suggest when you arrived.'

'No, Miss Warren. You misunderstand. The mystery is why someone should send us a copy.'

'But there's no mystery there either, is there? Somebody's trying to put you off the scent. It's a diversion, a decoy, a complete red herring.'

'So you have theories about Fr Wilfred's death?'

'Certainly: I don't sit here all day knitting, you know, Inspector. No, I think, and of course I've been thinking about why anyone should wish to murder the poor man. Now how it was done is your business: I'm more than glad to leave that to you. You policeman have ways and means of working out little problems like that, and I hope you haven't forgotten my little reference to Heyer. No, I've been working on the motive or motives behind the murder.'

'And my I ask what you have come up with?'

'Certainly you may ask, and I can tell you why my uncle's pamphlet has nothing to do with it. My uncle floated the idea that in certain cases unsuitable pastors could be removed, by force if necessary, but that has absolutely nothing to do with Fr Wilfred. He wasn't an unsuitable pastor. He was a holy man, a sincere man of God. He would be retiring in a few years anyway, and the parish was managing to get along.'

'So progressive elements in the parish had nothing to do with his death?'

'Good heavens, whatever put that idea into your head? No, no, nothing of the kind.'

Here she paused, and Wickfield prompted her.

'So why was he killed, then?'

Miss Warren leaned forward and adjusted her voice to a whisper.

'I've told you before, Gentlemen: an infiltrator. I don't know who, but he's from one of those funny sects with an anti-Catholic mania who thought he was doing the world a favour by removing Catholic leaders.'

'But Fr Wilfred wasn't a leader.'

'Oh, but he was – in Droitwich!'

There not seeming much to be said after that, Wickfield and Spooner, thanking Miss Warren for her time and her suggestion, which they promised to consider further, took their leave. Wickfield thought they should pay a courtesy visit to Fr Gabriel, as they were in the town, and a few minutes after saying farewell to the erudite admirer of Voltaire and d'Azeglio, they rang the bell at the presbytery. Slightly to their surprise, the door was opened by a much older priest than Fr Gabriel.

'Good morning, Gentlemen, welcome to the Sacred Heart. What can I do for you?'

'Er, we're detectives from Worcester, and we've been inquiring into Fr Wilfred's death. We were hoping to have a word with Fr Gabriel.'

'Yes, of course, come in, come in. My name's Hugh Griffin, by the way, and I've taken Fr Wilfred's place, at least for the time being.'

The two visitors were shown into the by now familiar sitting-room, and soon Fr Gabriel joined them. Fr Griffin was clearly anxious to stay, and Wickfield saw no reason to gainsay him. Fr Gabriel looked much more himself: rested, relaxed, in the pink, if that phrase can be applied to one relatively dark skinned. The priests seemed to think that some explanation was required. The curate took the lead.

'After your visit to Saltley last night, Inspector, the VG came rushing over all of a flutter, obviously concerned that I was heading for the funny farm or possibly going to do away with myself. We talked, and the upshot was that I spent the night at Saltley but came over here first thing this morning to help Fr Griffin get settled. I think he realised that he shouldn't have left me on my own in the parish with occasional help from Oscott, so Fr Griffin is now a fixture, at least a temporary one.'

'Well, I'm delighted to hear it, Father. You look better already!' and then turning to the older priest, Wickfield asked,

'Has Fr Gabriel filled you in yet on our investigation?'

'No, not at all. I've only just arrived – well, an hour ago - and I've been finding my feet. We were going to sit down after lunch to go over things. What ought I to know?'

'Well, we'll leave Fr Gabriel to give you his side of the story, obviously, but we really popped in this morning to tell Fr Gabriel the result of a conversation we've just had with Miss Tabitha Warren down the road.'

Fr Griffin looked at Fr Gabriel.

'Miss Warren is a choir member and one of the more learned and active members of the parish, Father,' he explained. 'She's quite a character. Born and brought up here, way back in the last century!'

'Now, Gentlemen,' continued Wickfield, 'please keep all this under your hat, at least for the moment. We can't have rumours or accusations flying round the parish and doing possibly a great deal of damage. I know I can rely on your discretion. Yesterday morning, we received through the post a booklet – part of a booklet - written by an anonymous priest of the diocese in 1908. Fr Gabriel will tell you what's in it, Father,' he said to the new parish priest. 'This morning we called on Miss Warren, as a remark made by her some time ago suggested to me that she might be able to help us. Well, it turns out that it was written by her uncle. *That* surprised us, I can tell you! Now she has another theory about the murder. She thinks the booklet is a complete non-starter: a red herring altogether. No, her idea is that a Non-Conformist Protestant, if I've understood her correctly, is carrying out some sort of anti-Catholic reprisal, and that he's an unbalanced religious maniac. That's the general drift of her theory, would you agree, Sergeant?'

'Yes, Sir.'

'Now do you think there can be any truth in it? Unfortunately, she couldn't tell us how the murder was committed by a deranged Protestant in a quiet Catholic church during confessions.'

There was a knock on the sitting-room door, and a head but no body appeared. It was Basil Jennings.

'Sorry to interrupt, Fathers. I heard voices and thought I'd ask if anyone knew where the petty-cash box had gone. It's time I replaced the vase that got broken on the evening of Fr Wilfred's death.'

Fr Gabriel made as if to speak, but Inspector Wickfield forestalled him.

'You mean a vase was broken during confessions?'

'Yes, it was.'

'Which vase, where?'

'The one at the foot of the Lady statue. One of the women accidentally brushed it off the pedestal as she leaned over to light a candle. It wasn't an expensive one, but we haven't got another. I'm off down to the market and thought I'd get a cheap one.'

'When abouts during confessions?'

'Right towards the end,' Jennings answered. 'I didn't have time to sweep it up, so I just nudged the pieces under the candle-rack with my foot.'

'But why wasn't this repeated at the reconstruction we staged on Saturday?'

'What, you wanted the poor woman to break *another* vase?'

'I should have been told,' Wickfield lamented. 'It puts quite a different complexion on things,' but he could see from the blank looks on the others' faces, including Spooner's, that no one had grasped his point.

'Who was the woman who broke the vase, do you know?'

'Yes,' Jennings said, 'although I can't for the life of me see what difference it makes. It was Mrs Ryan.'

Fr Gabriel rose from his chair with an apology and went out with Jennings, returning a moment later to resume the discussion in the sitting-room.

'So,' the inspector said, resuming the thread of his argument, but clearly still turning over Jennings' news in his mind, 'could Miss Warren be right? We're not thinking of a parishioner at all, we're thinking of an anti-Catholic from outside the parish but presumably from Droitwich town. What do you think, Fr Gabriel?'

'Miss Warren's theory throws the whole business wide open, doesn't it? Far from narrowing your list of suspects down to a few, you've extended it to encompass virtually the entire population of Great Britain – and Northern Ireland too, I suppose. There must be dozens of anti-Catholic maniacs out there just waiting for an opportunity to take a clergyman out.'

'Well,' Wickfield insisted, 'I don't think that's necessarily the case. On our preliminary analysis, this wasn't a random killing executed by an opportunist. This was a carefully planned operation. I feel I ought to tell you now, Fathers, that someone tampered with the grille at the altar end of the confessional, so that it could be lifted out and replaced with the minimum of effort. It would be a matter of seconds to remove the grille, stab the priest and put the grille back. I tried it on Sunday, when the church had emptied at the end of the last Mass, and it took me four seconds; you couldn't tell afterwards that the grille had been disturbed.'

The priests looked at him dumbfounded.

'However, I could be quite wrong. Mr Jennings' little intervention changes things entirely: perhaps we *are* thinking of an unhinged, murderous, diabolical enemy of the Church stalking Droitwich and sticking daggers into harmless priests. We must go away and do some more thinking! But before we do that, I have one further question for Fr Gabriel. The autopsy on Fr Wilfred discovered traces of phenobarbital in his blood: do you know why he was taking it, or for how long?'

'No, I didn't know he was, although during the last week of his life I thought he seemed a bit agitated, as if something were on his mind. I did ask him whether he felt all right, and he dismissed my question with a "Yes, of course". It's just possible Mrs Gould might know.'

Wickfield and Spooner asked Fr Gabriel, finally, for the two Worcester schools where Thomas Foynes worked as a laboratory assistant and for Mrs Ryan's address and left the presbytery.

When they were back at the car, Spooner asked his superior to explain to him why the breaking of the vase had seemed to excite his interest so: he himself could not see its relevance. Wickfield explained.

'The Lady statue is a third of the way down the church on the left hand side, more or less opposite the confessional, and the candle-stand is just next to it. Imagine you were sitting in church that evening. Everything is hushed. In the silence there is a smash of breaking glass. What do you do? You turn your head to look: it's instinctive, you do it automatically. In the half-light you strain to glimpse the cause of the noise, and you pick out Mrs Ryan with her hands to her mouth. You imagine her embarrassment and you contemplate going to see whether you can help. At that moment Basil Jennings appears at the door of the sacristy to discover the cause of the disturbance, and he potters down the church to kick the offending pieces of glass under the stand and to reassure Mrs Ryan that all is now well. Now I've doubtless dramatised it a bit, but we can imagine something like that happening, can't we?'

'Yes, Sir, and so?'

'Good heavens, Spooner, don't you see it yet? For a few seconds, all eyes would be on the Lady statue; and that means that no eyes were on the confessional. Now Jennings told us that this little incident – too small, apparently, to warrant inclusion in our little re-enactment – took place towards the end of the session. What better cover could our killer have for his murder than a diversion on the far side of the church? Mrs Ryan is his accomplice. At a prearranged time, or at a given signal, she accidentally on purpose tips the vase over and creates a little bit of a fuss. Fr Wilfred is done to death. By the time the vase incident is over, the killer has disappeared, and nobody even remembers he was there. This means we can return to your original idea, that Fr Wilfred was killed by someone standing *outside* the confessional. Miss Warren is right, in that case: the unseated grille is a red herring. This is all very mysterious.'

Ten

*T*he immediate task was to interview Thomas Foynes and Mrs Ryan. The investigating team could explore the fanatical, murderous and possibly deranged Protestant aspect later if it should prove necessary. Spooner caught up with Thomas Foynes in the chemistry laboratory at Nunnery Wood Secondary School, as he was clearing up after an O-level chemistry practical. Spooner's own school days were not far distant, and he remembered his chemistry practicals with distaste. However, he was not to let that colour his interview with Mr Foynes. Pupils wandering about looked at the policeman askance, but the two were eventually closeted privately enough in the Prep Room, as it was reasonably called. Since their last encounter, at the meeting of the Third World Aid group, Mr Foynes had found time to shave. He was still thin and balding, of course, but clean-shaven he made a more prepossessing impression on the detective sergeant. In any case, Spooner found difficulty in seeing Foynes – devout, politically aware, alleged would-be candidate for the priesthood – as the murderer of a man he professed to admire. Spooner, instructed by his superior neither to antagonise nor to accuse his man, trod warily.

'Mr Foynes, I'm sorry, it's me again! Yes, we're still investigating. Please carry on with your work. May I first of all just put to you what might seem an irrelevant question: did you ever consider the Catholic priesthood?'

'Yes, I did: not straightaway after school, but in my mid-twenties I made inquiries and applied.'

'This was to what I understand you call the secular priesthood?'

'Yes.'

'And why didn't you go ahead?'

'I believe that the parish priest gave an unflattering assessment of my personal qualities.'

'is that what you were told?'

'Well, not in those words. I had a letter back from the archbishop saying that he very much appreciated my interest but that he was bound to take into consideration the opinion of the local clergy, and in Fr Tarbuck's estimation I should not be happy in the priesthood.'

'Well, couldn't they have allowed you to give it a try? They could have weeded you out subsequently if Fr Tarbuck's opinion was found to be justified.'

'In theory, yes, Sergeant, but I did not deny being gay – why should I? – and that obviously excluded me from the outset. I suppose if I'd been less honest …`

'Did you ever hold it against Fr Wilfred?'

'Is that supposed to be a motive for murder, Sergeant?' he asked with a grin. Spooner felt a bit uncomfortable.

'I'm afraid you can't wonder at being a suspect, Mr Foynes, as you were the last person to speak with Fr Wilfred.'

'Yes, well, I certainly didn't kill him, as I've told you before. And the answer to your question is that, no, I didn't hold it against him. My sexuality would have come out sooner or later anyway, and I suppose it was more comfortable for me, and for everyone else, if I never started at Oscott. I have no regrets. I swallowed the pill as a divine gift, and here I am still!'

'How well do you know Miss Tabitha Warren?'

'Not really very well. Of course, I know who she is: hardly anyone in Droitwich doesn't, but I've not spoken to her very often or very much. Why?'

'Oh, nothing. In a way, all those who went to confession that evening, and those who were in the church, are suspects. Have you any views on the murder yourself?'

'No, I'm leaving that to you people! I've got enough to worry about as it is.'

While this interview was in progress, Wickfield was interviewing Mrs Bridie Ryan at her home in Leigh Grove, Droitwich. Leigh Grove backs on to the river, but Wickfield did not feel that that enhanced the road's aspect. However, he reminded himself that he was not sightseeing and that he was facing a tricky assignation. In the event, his fears proved groundless. Mrs Ryan, housewife, answered the door in her pinafore and welcomed him in. He accepted a cup of tea, keen to quench the thirst that had built up since lunch, and the two of them sat comfortably in the kitchen. Mrs Ryan excused the venue on the pretext that, since she was at that very moment engaged in cleaning the living-room, the latter room was a 'bit of a mess'.

'You were at the reconstruction of Fr Wilfred's murder on Saturday, Mrs Ryan. Why didn't you break a vase again? I had asked everybody to repeat their movements exactly.'

She laughed.

'I was that embarrassed the first time, Inspector, I would hardly want to do it again! In any case, I had forgotten all about it. I suppose I could have bought a cheap vase, knocked it off the pedestal and blushed, but what would have been the good of that? It could hardly have any bearing on poor Father's death.'

'Tell me how you managed it.'

'The vase – a tall, hexagonal thing in plain glass – was at the foot of the Lady statue full of cut flowers and foliage. I saw one of the candles just singeing the bottom leaves and thought it wasn't quite safe. I mean, nothing could have caught fire, I see that now, but at the time I just leant over to move the candle a bit to one side. My elbow or my sleeve must have caught the vase, and over it went. That's all there was to it. I felt such a fool.'

'What did you do?'

'I stood there for a minute, wondering whether to make more fuss by calling for a dustpan and brush or just to walk away and leave it, when Mr Jennings, God bless him, came to my assistance and took over. It was nothing, Inspector, all over in a half-a-minute and certainly not worth repeating on Saturday.'

'Mrs Ryan, I'm going to be quite candid with you. While your scene was going on, we think someone may have used the diversion as an opportunity to murder Fr Wilfred and make good his escape.'

'What? It was a cover for murder? You've got to be joking!'

Wickfield was unaccountably put out by this jocular reaction to his serious proposal, and he began to view Mrs Ryan in a less than sympathetic light.

'Well, perhaps you have a better theory yourself for how someone managed to stab Fr Wilfred in the confessional?'

'No, I've no better theory. I've no theory at all. To be honest with you, Inspector, I'd never regarded the mechanics of the murder as a problem: just never thought about it.'

'What was your opinion of Fr Wilfred?'

'Do you mean, did I want him dead? No, not at all. He was a bit of an old buffer, but we could have had worse parish priests: you should see some of them in the archdiocese! Crikey, some priests are really odd, or perhaps I shouldn't be saying that. But no, Fr Wilfred was more or less harmless, particularly as he let Fr Gabriel get on with the job.'

'Did he, though?'

'Well, of course, I understand there were tensions, because Fr W was an old stick-in-the-mud and Fr G wanted to get things moving, but Fr G did pretty well, considering. We'll just have to see how he gets on with the new man, whatever his name is.'

Wickfield was understandably disappointed by the result of this interview, even though it helped to the extent of excluding, at least provisionally, one theory amongst the many on which they had been working. Perhaps he would have more success with his unhinged, maverick Protestant on the loose in Droitwich with a dagger up his sleeve.

First of all he spent time at the public library in Droitwich looking up the Churches and Christian groups in the town: necessarily limited in a settlement of only 7000 souls. He discounted the Anglican Churches, for two reasons, neither of which might have satisfied a more rigorous researcher. Firstly, Anglicans of the twentieth century do not have a recent tradition of assassinating Roman Catholics. Secondly, relations between the Church of England and the Church of Rome in the town seemed, particularly in the light of Fr Gabriel's efforts in that direction, reasonably cordial. One could not, of course, discount maverick members. He also discounted the main-stream Non-Conformist Churches in the town: the Methodists, the Baptists, the Salvation Army. He reasoned that such groups were not a hotbed of anti-Catholic polemic: their disagreements with Rome, biblically based, deeply felt and sincere though they were, were more likely to be argued to than imposed at the tip of a dagger. This left just three groups whom Wickfield thought of (layman though he was in these matters) as theologically and historically marginal: the Church of the Gospellers, Election Covenanters and the Lord's Associates. These groups – groupuscules! – belonged respectively to the Lutheran, Calvinist and Zwinglian traditions, and Wickfield knew at once that he was out of his depth. To give himself a vague idea of what he was up against, he called on Fr Henry Bancks at Oscott once again. This time the college was bathed in weak sunshine. The grounds were trim and attractive, and he thought that there were far worse places on earth where one might spend six years engaged in placid if intense study. He was received in Fr Banck's study, on the ground floor at the front of the college, overlooking the terrace, the woods beyond and the city beyond that. This was a civilised space! He contrasted his life in pursuit of the delinquent and the crooked with that of a college lecturer closed off from the city and surrounded by his books and his prayers. Ah, well!

Wickfield gave the very briefest account of his needs.

'We're working on several fronts at once,' he said, 'trying to establish how the murder was committed, by whom and for what reason. One of our theories, which is not necessarily either the correct one or the most attractive, is that poor Fr Wilfred was killed by a local person with a resentment against the Catholic Church. In this context, he was killed not for who he was in himself but merely for what he stood for. Now for various reasons with which I shall not bore you here, Father, we have chosen to focus on three small, rabidly Protestant groups in the town, and it's those I want you to tell me about, in the very briefest compass.'

'That's a very tall order, Inspector. You see, Protestantism is of its very nature fissiparous. If the norms of your belief are Scripture and your own interpretation of it in the light of your experience and divine guidance, what you believe ends up being what you feel is right. I don't wish to sound critical here, because I'm not. Protestants tend to regard the fragmentation of Reformed Christianity as one of its strengths. There are hundreds and hundreds of Protestant sects: probably thousands, some numbering a handful of likeminded people, others being considerable Churches. The important thing is your relationship to God, not whether you belong to a mainstream Church or not. What I'm really telling you is that no one person can master all the shades of difference among the Protestant Churches and sects.'

'No, I quite understand that,' Wickfield said. 'What I want is thumbnail sketches of three small groups that belong respectively to the Lutheran, Calvinist and Zwinglian traditions.'

'Ah,' said Fr Bancks, 'thumbnail sketches! The best one I've ever heard, although it's quite irrelevant here, is one about the great Reformed theologian Karl Barth, who must be well into his eighties by now but still writing. This is how it goes:

God is everything.

I am nothing.

And you are a fool.

It's brilliant because it encapsulates the man and his theology concisely and wittily. Oh, sorry, Inspector, this isn't what you came to hear! My apologies. Right. Three thumbnail sketches coming up. Droitwich. I'm ignoring your particular groups, because I know nothing about them, but here's some general background information first. Protestants protest. The Catholic Church had got everything wrong. From the fourth century onwards, there had been a steady decline, and putrefaction had set in in virtually every aspect of Christian life and worship. What to do about it? Reform! Start where you like, but gradually work your way through the various aspects of Christianity and bring about change. Leave nothing untouched until you are certain of having got back to the original ideals. That's Protestantism, in a nutshell. How am I doing?'

'Very well so far, Father!'

'Good. But of course your particular interest is in how a member of your Churches would view Catholicism: the Harlot of Rome, the Whore of Babylon, the Scarlet Woman *par excellence*! OK, how's this? The three reformers in which you're interested were very different characters. Luther was a Saxon peasant, an Augustinian monk, who was in his early thirties when he nailed his *Theses* up in public in 1517. A wily *bon viveur*. Zwingli was a middle-class Swiss priest, a scholar and humanist, who anticipated Luther's criticism by several years: open-minded, politically liberal. He died in battle in 1531 at the age of forty-seven. Calvin was the son of a northern French lawyer, and he was twenty-seven when he published his famous *Institutes* in 1536: dour, puritanical, authoritarian. May I just ask what religion or denomination you are, Inspector?'

'Anglican, practising.'

'Well, perhaps I shouldn't be telling you this, but you're broad-minded enough not to take offence! We jokingly divide the Anglican Church into three: high and crazy, broad and hazy, low and lazy. Not very flattering, I'm afraid, but it's only in fun. Now that's how we can see your three reformers. Calvin is high and crazy: a fanatic, bitterly opposed to Rome. Zwingli is broad and hazy, decidedly against Rome but without Calvin's obsessive emphasis on purity of life and social homogeneity. Luther, finally, is low and lazy, anxious to clean Rome up, but neither a politician nor a dictator. Not very accurate, perhaps, but you did ask for sketches! Shall I go on?'

'Yes, please. I'm learning a great deal.'

'Well, where enmity to Rome is concerned, any Protestant, of whatever persuasion, is against us, but obviously some more convincedly and fervently than others. Do people take after the founders they follow? No, not at all, but it has always baffled me how anyone can follow Karl Marx, who was one of the most unpleasant men you would meet in a day's march. Compare him with the Jesus of the Gospels. Well, there is no comparison, and yet some prefer to entrust their lives to Marxism than to Christianity. Completely mystifying. However, I'm wandering from the point, aren't I? To sum up, then, any Protestant would gladly murder the Pope – I suppose – but a Calvinist is more likely to than a Lutheran, and a Zwinglian could zwing either way. How's that?'

'Wonderful, Father, it's not given me many answers, but it's put me in the picture.'

'Just let me make one more comment, although it properly belongs to my colleagues in the social sciences than to me as a historian, I suppose. If you're mentally touched, slightly odd, theologically eccentric, liturgically weird or socially unconventional, you're more likely to end up in a small sect than in a main-stream denomination. Sects have a habit of gathering misfits – or so it seems to me.'

Wickfield, appreciating even on such short acquaintance the lecturer's willingness to talk and instruct, his historian's sense of balance, his courtesy to his opponents without loss of his own convictions, his ability to encapsulate in digestible morsels acres of fact, envied the college students their opportunities. How is it, then, that some of those who had studied under such wise and learned men had allowed their conservatism to take hold and develop into intransigent traditionalism? He recalled a definition he had heard years before: tradition is not what is handed down; it is what is handed over. In other words, its reference is not to the past – what should be preserved – but to the present and future – what is valued enough to be passed on to sympathetic inquirers and to the next generation. It does not shackle; it liberates. It does not mindlessly transmit; it requires all the material to be sifted and assessed. He also remembered a phrase of Quiller-Couch's about his character Richard Montgomery (although he could not remember the name of the book in which it occurred[*]): he was 'very little concerned with religion,' comments the author, 'beyond damning the Pope'. One did not have to be a religious maniac to wish to eliminate the leader of the Roman Church. However, it was now time to advance to the next stage of his inquiry.

He telephoned through to the station to ask them to pass the message on to Spooner that the sergeant was to join him in Droitwich. They met in a town-centre café and refreshed the inner man with a pot of tea and a bun, whilst Wickfield briefed his sergeant on the evening's work that faced them. The pastor (if that was the correct nomenclature) of the Church of the Gospellers, a vaguely Lutheran group, was a certain Mrs Doris Healey, who lived modestly (if her house and furnishings were any indication) with her husband and two teenage children on the edge of the town, in Mosel Drive. She did not fit the profile offered tentatively by Fr Bancks, but impressed the inspector and his sergeant with her normality and sanity. She was, Wickfield supposed, in her late thirties or early forties, a buxom, homely creature, with a motherly, no-nonsense feel to her. The men found her deep in preparations for the evening meal with the family, apologised and assured her that they would not

---

[*] *Fort Amity*, 1912, chapter 1. JF.

keep her long.

'Mrs Healey,' Wickfield began, 'you will know that Fr Wilfred Tarbuck, of the Sacred Heart Roman Catholic parish in the town, was stabbed to death ten days ago, and we think you may be able to help.'

'Who, me? Come off it, Inspector, I never met the man. I used to see a Roman collar in the town, and I suppose that's who it was, but I never spoke to him in my life. What would I know about his murder, for heaven's sake?'

'Please bear with us, Mrs Healey. One theory that has been put to us' – by the colourful and perhaps fanciful Miss Warren, only he did not of course disclose this – 'is that some anti-Catholic element in the town might have been responsible: not a personal enemy of the priest, you understand, but an enemy of his Church. Now we're asking round important religious groups in Droitwich to see whether such an enemy is known and can be identified – for purposes of elimination, if nothing else. So we have come to you for assistance. You have your ear to the ground. Has anyone ever expressed to you such bitter hatred of Popish ways that murder might be on his mind?'

'I know what you're thinking, Inspector,' said Mrs Healey. 'You're saying to yourself, I wonder whether that crackpotted Church of the Gospellers, with the eccentric Mrs Healey as its organiser, nourishes in its bosom a lunatic capable of murder.'

Seeing that denial would be counterproductive, Wickfield decided to laugh with her.

'How perspicacious of you, Mrs Healey. I didn't know I was so transparent!'

'Oh, don't worry, Inspector, it's a reaction we often get. I don't mind a bit. No, we're quite serious in our religion, but none of the main Churches seems to suit us. We do things quietly in our own way.'

'So, what is the answer to my question?'

'I can't speak for the wider community, of course, you see that, but within our own Church, there's absolutely no one who would fit your description. Rome is nothing to us. That's about all I can say.'

Wickfield and Spooner moved on to their second target, a Mr Wallace Smith, who resided in the delightfully named Nine Foot Way in the town, a quiet cul-de-sac that backed on to Saltway and provided this particular resident with a haven from his labours as a county surveyor. Wickfield was surprised that, as a clearly educated man, Mr Smith had elected to be a member of, indeed the pastor of, the Lord's Associates, but he rebuked himself for such a patronising and probably ill-informed attitude. Although he straightened his mind so that he could meet the man with his usual courtesy and poise, he asked Spooner to conduct the interview.

'Mr Smith,' the latter began, 'you will know from your newspapers of the murder of the Roman Catholic priest in the town ten days ago.'

'Of course, Sergeant, and a very regrettable affair it was. I bear no love for our Roman neighbours, but I wouldn't wish that on anyone: struck down in cold blood as he was going about his business. Dearie me, what a world we live in!'

'Quite, Sir, but we've come to you for a bit of information.'

'To me? I don't know anything about it. Why on earth should I?'

'The thing is this, Sir. Somebody has proposed the theory that he was killed for being a representative of the Roman Catholic community in Droitwich –`

' – and you think one of us is crazed enough to do it!'

'Well, not exactly that, but you might know someone who was. As a pastor, you get about a good deal. I daresay you're in touch with a lot of religious people in the town, and well, you know...' He faded away rather lamely.

'Why do you people think that, just because we're a small group, we're nutters? The nutters are those who persist with worn-out forms of service and tired creeds. Why don't these people join us in the twentieth century? Go and look for your murderer in the pews of St Michael's or perhaps in the grottier reaches of the Marxist-Leninist-Trotskyist United Workers' Up the 7 November Down-with-the-Pope Federation. They're a much likelier bet!'

'Just as a matter of interest, Sir, and I hope you'll forgive the question in a right spirit of public service, where were you on the evening of 8 February, between the hours of six-thirty and seven?'

'Good heavens, Sergeant, you're not suggesting ...?'

Wickfield intervened.

'It's a question we have to ask, Sir. It implies nothing.'

'I don't know where I was.'

'Perhaps you'd be good enough to check your diary, Sir,' Spooner said with as much politeness as he could muster.

Mr Smith had a cast-iron alibi, but the detectives had lost his thin allowance of goodwill.

The third person on their list was the leader of the Election Covenanters, a Mr Bertram Eton, who lived near the railway station in Ombersley Road. (What had possessed the town fathers, Wickfield wondered, to have an Ombersley Way, an Ombersley Road, an Ombersley Street West and an Ombersley Street East? There must be easier and less confusing methods of naming streets!) He was a giant of a man, with a mop of red hair and long red side-burns and stains down his waistcoat. Wickfield immediately had him down as a butcher (although in this he was mistaken). Quite why butchery and Calvinism should be ill-matched in Wickfield's mind he could not fathom. From his accent, Wickfield divined that Mr Eton hailed, as he half-expected, from 'the knuckle-end of England – that land of Calvin, oat-cakes, and sulphur', but Mr Eton was not a whit sulphurous. On the contrary, he was jovial whilst evincing an underlying seriousness of purpose: a finely tuned combination. Wickfield was impressed. On the other hand, there was something very odd or quirky about him which disconcerted but which Wickfield could not rightly analyse. Wickfield explained the purpose of their visit.

'What all that boils down to, Inspector,' Eton commented, 'is that you don't think an Anglican or a Roman capable of murdering so misguided and dangerous a man as Tarbuck, but some cranky Scottish sectarian is. That's about it, isn't it? You look at us, dismiss us as lunatics on the fringe and say to yourself, Yep, they're just about capable of anything. Don't you realise just how damaging to society the doctrines of Rome are? Out of Rome come all sorts of lies, profanity, immorality, godlessness and devilry, turning the world away from God and driving it into Satan's clutches. The Pope and his evil minions twist the Bible to suit their own ends, shamefully misrepresent St Paul, fly in the face of truth and damage our children beyond repair. The Reformation was only a start: the work has to go on, generation by generation, until Rome's falsehoods and deceits are crushed for ever. Yes, I'd like to have strangled Tarbuck myself, to put an end to his absurd posturings and endless stream of filth – but I didn't, and neither did any of my flock. The Bible instructs us to hate evil, to shun the evildoer, to strain every nerve to counter the wiles of Satan - but also to respect life.'

During this little speech, Eton had quite worked himself up into a lather of fury, but as he ended, his calmer side reappeared for a second. He continued almost immediately with a Cobbett-style rant.

'You see, Gentlemen,' he said, 'Calvin was absolutely right that where the state is not governed by Christian principles as set out in the Bible, the way is open to every sort of aberration and immorality. You've only to look at the society around us' – and he waved a stout, hairy arm in a wide sweep to take in, seemingly, the whole of Britain and probably Europe as well – 'to appreciate the horrors of Popery: swindles, drugs, teenage pregnancy, murders and rapes, wars and child abuse, drink and sex – you name it! There is no discipline in our leaders and therefore no discipline in society, and that's because the likes of Tarbuck peddle a devilish creed putting power into the hands of little men who base their teaching not on the Bible but on the man-made traditions of Rome! It's all self, you see, not the Lord above.'

'Could we just ask where you were on the evening of Thursday 8 February, Mr Eton, between the hours of half-past six and seven o-clock? Please don't take offence: you must understand that we have to ask these questions.'

'No, I don't mind you asking, although I've already told you I had nothing to do with Tarbuck's murder. Last Thursday? I was here, preparing for our usual midweek meeting.'

Wickfield and Spooner felt they could decently, without giving offence to one who was sincere but fanatical (if that word did not betray their own prejudices), take their leave at this point. Their heads span. The inspector instructed his sergeant to reconvene in the morning so that they could consider matters calmly in the light of what they had learnt in the course of a long day's talking and listening. As it turned out, their consideration of matters was slightly delayed by more urgent concerns.

Eleven

Wickfield had not forgotten that one small thread he had not yet examined was Fr Wilfred's recent medical history. He did not set great store by the priest's use of phenobarbital, but feeling that he ought at least to simulate some sort of inquiry in that direction, he decided to consult Dr Gus Moore, the late priest's physician in Droitwich. Dr Moore was a good-humoured, rotund man of forty, nattily dressed in a brown tweed suit with purple shirt and matching tie. His surgery waiting-room was a model of respectability and ease, designed to coax his patients into a suitable frame of mind. It is sometimes said that medical men – at least general practitioners – fall into one of two categories: the learned and the comfortable. The former know their stuff but lack ease of manner, while the latter compensate for their relative lack of medical erudition by an engaging style which heals by soothing. If there is any justice in this assessment, Wickfield judged that Dr Moore fell into the second category.

'Dr Moore,' he said, 'I'm sorry to be troubling you, particularly as I cannot assure you of the relevance of my inquiry, but I thought I ought to take the opportunity to consult you briefly on Fr Tarbuck's recent medical history. He died of a stab wound to the chest, as you may be aware, but the pathologist also reported the presence of phenobarbital, and I wondered what you could tell me about that.'

'No, you're not troubling me at all, Inspector. I'm happy to help out if I can. A couple of months back, Fr Wilfred came to see me because he was worried about an increasing forgetfulness. Now of course there could be various causes of that, and I thought it best to refer him to a specialist. The report came back that the psycho-geriatrician diagnosed the lower slopes of vascular dementia and advised stimulating mental activity daily to counteract the more extreme manifestations of poor memory. He didn't think drugs would do any good; and the outlook was not very bright. I went over the report with Fr Wilfred, and I could see at a glance that the diagnosis, as well it might, hit him hard. He told me that he had hoped to see out at least another seven years, until his seventy-fifth birthday, particularly important, he thought, in the light of increasing tensions in the Church. I asked him about this, and he sketched in for me the difficulties being experienced by some of the older laity, as well as older clergy like himself, in combatting what they saw as a wave of vandalism and experimentation in the wake of the Second Vatican Council. Of course, I couldn't comment on that at all, being not just a non-Catholic but an unbeliever, but after some conversation, I prescribed a mild sedative to try to calm his chief anxieties.'

'Forgive my asking, Doctor,' Wickfield said as a thought struck him, 'would you say that Fr Tarbuck was in any way suicidal?'

'Ooh, that's a hard one to answer! He was certainly depressed by the news, but suicidal? I really can't say. If he had committed suicide, I shouldn't have been surprised, let me put it that way, except that I understand suicide is frowned on by his Church.'

Wickfield came away full of a new possibility. Was it at all feasible that Fr Wilfred had committed suicide in the confessional and that a well-meaning parishioner had walked off with the weapon so that self-harm would not be suspected? Would that cohere with the facts? He put this question to his assistant.

'Crikey, Inspector, that's a novel analysis! Let's for one moment imagine it's true.' He paused to collect a few thoughts. 'What about this? The last penitent, Mr Foynes, somehow realises that the confessor is at the end of his tether and has purposed to do away with himself. Perhaps something in their conversation persuaded the priest to unburden himself. Foynes immediately remonstrates with the priest, but to no avail. As he leaves the confessional, in a state of horror, shock and disbelief, he looks in on the priest – this moment coincides with the accidental breakage of a flower-vase on the other side of the church – takes in the situation at a glance, picks up the dagger, which is still clutched in the priest's hand, or lying on his lap, and makes off with it. His purpose is to spare the priest any sort of shame or dishonour in his final moments. The only person who could be suspected of murder is himself, and he knows he's innocent.'

'Right, Sergeant, that's a very good try, but tell me this: why would Fr Wilfred choose the confessional in which to commit suicide? Doesn't that strike you as excessively odd?'

'Well, there are two answers to that, Sir, although of course I'm not sure they're sufficient, even in combination. The first is that we cannot see into the mind of a desperate man: there is no knowing how he might see things or feel in his desperation. The second answer is that perhaps it was the confessional where he felt most vulnerable to his recently diagnosed condition. His forgetfulness or absent-mindedness leads him to forget what the penitent has said, or what he himself should say next, and he thinks that his penitential ministry is drawing to a rapid close, in full view, so to speak, of his parishioners.'

'OK,' Wickfield said slowly, digesting this breakdown of the priest's state of mind. 'Tell me what the priest was doing with a stiletto in his pocket.'

'What if it was a kitchen knife? He had forgotten his appointment with his son; he was in the middle of slicing carrots or potatoes for his evening meal; he suddenly sees the time – he ought to be hearing confessions before Benediction - and hastens into the sacristy, pushing the knife into his pocket.'

'Mm, I wonder,' the inspector said thoughtfully. 'How could we ever prove that? Thomas Foynes is going to continue to cover up, and he will have got rid of the knife days ago. It's a puzzle, that's for sure, but it would certainly save us a wild goose chase for a criminal who doesn't exist. I tell you what, Sergeant: this case is getting me down! So many imponderables, so many possibilities, so many suspects – or none at all! What are we to make of it?'

They were saved further thought on the subject immediately by a telephone-call put through by the switchboard from Oscott College.

'Inspector, I hope this call is not inappropriate. It's Henry Bancks at Oscott, and I have a confession to make.'

'What: not concealing relevant information from the police, I hope?' Wickfield said jocularly.

'No, no, nothing like that, Inspector. You know us priests: law-abiding in every respect, model citizens and so forth. No, it's just that I've been doing a modest bit of sleuthing myself.'

'Tell me more,' said Wickfield. 'I'm intrigued: sleuthing in the dimly-lit corridors of a major seminary!'

'After our last conversation, I was puzzled as to how a pamphlet written in 1908 by an anonymous priest could have any bearing on the murder of a priest in 1968, so last night I did a little rummaging in the library. It took me some time to run to earth what I was looking for. You see, as in any other library, books have to be signed out. It's not that we don't trust the students, but the librarian needs to know where every volume is, and the system is some sort of protection against theft. This is particularly important where our rarer books are concerned. So last night I went back over the signing-out jotters, and I was successful.' Wickfield could discern a modest chuckle down the line. 'I found an entry from three years ago,' the lecturer continued, 'which justified my efforts. On 4 March 1965 the college's only copy of *Bloodletting in the Body Ecclesiastic* was loaned out for a week to a reader from Droitwich.'

'Yes, go on, Father,' Wickfield said, himself intrigued to hear what was coming next.

'The borrower was called Ross or possibly Russ – the handwriting is not very clear – with the initial C – or possibly G. He gave no detailed address, just the town. I checked with Fr Ford, the librarian, and he has no recollection of the transaction, but he assures me that the pamphlet would not have been released unless the borrower had given satisfactory proof of identity and residence. Not that the pamphlet was important in itself – it will probably never be read again – but it was the only copy in the library and is in any case of some historical interest to us. Anyhow, I thought you'd be interested.'

'I am, oh, indeed, I am! Thank you so much for your public spirit.'

'Of course, Inspector, I'm making no accusations, none at all. I don't know who the person might be, and he or she might in any case be perfectly innocent of any crime or criminal intent, but I thought it worth while to pass the information on to you.'

'Yes, indeed, it may prove a very valuable piece of evidence.'

Thus the investigating team found themselves faced with two repeat interviews, either of which might prove decisive. Thomas Foynes, if he were so minded, could support or lay to rest the hypothesis that Fr Wilfred had committed hara-kari in the confessional, and Christopher Ross could be led to confess that he was behind the dispatch of the subversive booklet to the police-station and so expose his intimate participation in recent events at the Sacred Heart. To speed up the investigation, Wickfield invited Spooner to approach Foynes, while he himself would pay a visit to Ross.

Spooner found Foynes at his other place of work, King's, on the river Severn in the heart of the city. He was looking harassed.

'Keep talking, Sergeant,' he said, 'but you must excuse me while I finish preparing the apparatus for this physics practical. If it's not ready, the head of department throws a wobbly, you see. Quite rightly, of course.'

'Would you prefer me to come back in ten or fifteen minutes?'

'No, not necessary, depending, of course, on what you've got on your mind.'

'Well, it's this,' Spooner said cautiously. 'We were wondering whether, after a day's consideration, you would care to modify the statement you made to me yesterday.'

'You mean alter it? Good heavens, why would I do that? The truth's the truth, you know, whether I tell you it yesterday or today.' He moved to a cupboard whence, with a clatter, he produced a dozen prisms.

'Well, in the meantime,' Spooner said, 'we've had occasion to review our understanding of Fr Wilfred's death. No, that's probably too strong a phrase. We've been wondering whether it was at all possible that he committed suicide.'

'Suicide? Goodness me, Sergeant, what an absurd idea. For a start, stabbing yourself in the side is a gruesome way to go, and to do it in the confessional, where he felt completely at one with his ministry: no, no, Sergeant, you're having me on.'

He paused, with a mirror in his hand. 'Actually, there's a curious aspect to that. Had it ever occurred to you that the wound which seemingly killed him reproduced the spear-thrust that the soldier made in Jesus' side on the cross? Now there's a thing!'

'And when did you see the wound?'

'In the presbytery living-room. The doctor opened up the priest's cassock to take a look, and of course I was there.'

'And you say it was the same as the wound in Christ's side?'

'Yes, if we are to believe the Shroud of Turin, which I do.' Foynes had stopped working under the influence of this new idea, but he recollected himself and resumed his bustling.

'Well, that's very interesting, but what I really wanted to ask you,' Spooner continued, 'is whether you know more than you've told us so far.'

'And what "more" would that be?'

'Well, I'm hoping *you*'ll tell *us*.'

'Look, Sergeant, you'll have to be more explicit. I'm busy and can't follow your line of thought. What should I tell you that I haven't done already?'

'OK, let me put it like this. *If* Fr Wilfred took his own life, perhaps while you were still in the confessional, is it possible that you looked in on him to remove the weapon, to save the scandal?'

'It's possible, I suppose, but I didn't. I can assure you I left the box and returned straightaway to my place in the church.'

'Which was where?'

'Towards the front, on the epistle side. But I told you this before.'

'So you did, sorry, but that means you would have had to pass the front of the confessional.'

'Yes. So?'

'So you could have looked in on him.'

'Yes, I've already told you, Sergeant, I could have done but didn't. Now you really must excuse me, I'm getting behind with this job.'

Meanwhile, Wickfield was doing battle with Christopher Ross, retired bookmaker. Mr Ross occupied a modest villa in Ripple Road,

Droitwich, where he lived with his wife and pet poodle. Wickfield, received with politeness but a distinct lack of warmth, decided to broach the subject on his mind without preamble.

'Mr Ross, in March 1965, you borrowed from the library at Oscott College a copy of a booklet entitled *Bloodletting in the Body Ecclesiastic.*'

'Did I? Perhaps I did, perhaps I didn't.'

'Did you or didn't you?'

'Well, if you say I did, I did, didn't I, Inspector?' He smiled sourly.

'May I ask why?

'Yes, you may ask,' but he said nothing further.

'And what's the answer?'

'You won't believe me if I tell you, so what's the point?'

'Try me, Mr Ross. I'm pretty open-minded.'

'This is going to sound improbable. I know I look to you like a brainless oaf, but I have a more refined side.'

'Why shouldn't I believe you? I make no prejudgments.' Wickfield thought he detected a slight thawing in Mr Ross's attitude.

'Well, three years ago, a gang of us got together for a bit of a laugh. There was actually a serious side to it, and we learnt a lot as well as enjoying ourselves. Vatican II had not long concluded its deliberations, and the young curate we had then had been telling us about it from the pulpit. A few of us put our heads together to see what abuses in the Church we would wish to sort out at a council of our own. The idea was to take twelve abuses, one for each of the apostles, and trace their causes. This wasn't to criticise the Church but to identify systems or measures that would prevent a recurrence. Of course, none of us was a scholar, so we asked Fr David, who was the curate, to give us a bit of guidance and a helping hand. We met once a week for three months, each member of the group undertaking to introduce the discussion in turn. I can't say that the discussions were on a very high level – they wouldn't have satisfied the examiners at Oxford – but they were not frivolous, and they served a valuable purpose. One of the things Fr David told us was that from then on the voice of the laity was to be heard; we thought we could make a contribution.'

'And what sorts of things did you pick on?'

'I suppose our list included all the obvious abuses. Let me see whether I can remember them all:' – and he raised the fingers of one hand, numbering them off as he proceeded - 'the Albigensian crusade, the crusades in the Holy Land, the treatment of Jews over the centuries, the Spanish Inquisition, the treatment of heretics and schismatics over the ages, the Church's resistance to science, the Church's resistance to biblical developments, the Index of Forbidden Books, simony in all its forms, the clerical abuse of minors and the goings-on in the Vatican. Yes, I think that's the list. Of course, there were, unfortunately, lots more to choose from. Somebody wanted to do the division of the Americas between the colonising nations of Europe, supposedly for purposes of mission, but in reality for the aggressive exploitation and sometimes complete destruction of the indigenous peoples. Someone else wanted to do the failure of the Church to move any way towards a democratic structure. I remember Fr David telling us that Pius XII, in a radio message broadcast on Christmas Eve in 1944, I think it was, admitted that democracy was a fruit of the gospel. Of course it should be applied everywhere in the world except the Catholic Church! Vatican II didn't even mention the matter: to advocate democracy in the world's dictatorships and tyrannies might just lead to charges of hypocrisy! But we couldn't take everything on board: we began to feel that twelve was a good round number with an apostolic ring to it. Some of the sessions were heavier than others, depending on what books the members of the group had chosen for background, but it was all very democratic and easy-going and friendly.'

'And let me guess: you undertook to research the treatment of heretics and schismatics.'

'Right first time, Inspector!'

'And what sorts of remedies did you come up with?'

'You mean me personally, or the group as a whole?'

'The group as a whole.'

'I'm glad you asked that, Inspector, because you've homed in on the main purpose of the exercise. We all considered ourselves loyal members of the Church, but we were dismayed by the negative reaction that abuses of the official systems engendered in outsiders. Too often the hierarchy seemed to act like bookies: manipulating the system so that they were always on the winning side. Justice and truth don't come into it. To prevent the continuance of this injustice, we came up again and again with two sovereign remedies. Perhaps we were naïve. The first was to have women in high positions. We didn't think the Church would ever have been so belligerent and cruel and ruthless if women had been in charge. The second was to scrap or least severely curtail the clerical elite, or alternatively to extend married clergy from the eastern to the western Church. Married men at the top would have been more understanding and tolerant, readier to compromise, more nuanced altogether. As I say, perhaps we were naïve.'

'And did your little group do anything about what you agreed on?'

'We did. One of us wrote it up in summary form and sent it off to the archbishop.'

'And?'

'Oh, nothing. He acknowledged our letter in a polite one of his own, and that was the last we ever heard; but it was fun while it lasted.'

'May I ask how you first heard of the anonymous pamphlet you based your, er, talk on?'

'Yes, Fr David put it my way. He remembered seeing a copy of it at Oscott, and said I should apply to borrow it; which is what I did.'

'Did you ever buy a copy of your own?'

'No, no need to, was there? I got the college copy, made notes, and handed it back. It wasn't something I wanted to keep for ever.'

'So you have no idea who might have sent a copy to me earlier this week?'

'Did somebody do that? Well, I hope you enjoyed it, Inspector, but no, I haven't the faintest idea.'

Wickfield returned to his office to make a few telephone calls, and he had hardly settled himself in his tattered office chair when his telephone rang. The receptionist downstairs informed him that the Archbishop of Birmingham would like a few words.

'Yes, Your Grace, hello. Stan Wickfield here.'

'Inspector, this is just a quick call to make contact. I just haven't found the time in the last week to come and see you, so I thought I'd ring. I'm not disturbing you, am I?'

'No, not at all. I'm only cogitating on the case. We're at a bit of an impasse, to be honest.'

'Oh, I trust you implicitly, Inspector: you'll get there in the end, I'm sure, and of course you can rely on us to give any help you need. I understand your sergeant contacted the office some little time back, and we were able to tell you what we know about Fr Wilfred's career.'

'Yes, that was most helpful. We fleshed out the bones by consulting his sister and, er, his son.'

'Ah, I was coming to that, Inspector, and that's really why I phoned, to be honest. If you've spoken to Damian Fay, you'll know all about the arrangement the archdiocese came to with regard to placing Fr Wilfred close enough to Smethwick for visits – although the need for that has long passed - and so on. I'm glad to say that we have never had cause to regret the original decision to allow Fr Wilfred to proceed to ordination, despite his little lapse. An admirable priest. A model to all our younger clergy. Now it occurred to me that his death might – I say only "might" – reveal some other indiscretion. I mean, I've no idea what your investigation has uncovered or where it's heading, and I should hate to think that some cuckolded husband is at the bottom of the parish's present troubles, but one can never tell. Oh dear, what I'm trying to say is that I have absolutely no reason to believe that Fr Wilfred was not in every way an exemplary and pious priest, but on past form, you would hurt, but not surprise, me to tell me you have uncovered some other liaison.'

'No, Your Grace, I can assure you we haven't. Your confidence in Fr Wilfred, as far as I can tell so far, is entirely well-founded.'

'Good, good. But I did just wish to say that if you *should* turn up anything, shall we say, out of place, I hope you would do your very best to conceal it from the public eye. I really should hate the newspapers to get hold of anything scurrilous or scandalous: they'd make the most of it, you can be sure, and we can do without that. We live in uncertain times, you know, Inspector, and any hint of scandal can do us an immense amount of harm.'

When Wickfield came off the telephone, he was full of surmise: the archbishop's call had set him thinking in a quite novel direction, and he was not sure he felt comfortable with it. The phrase *bloodletting in the body ecclesiastic* recurred to his devious and suspicious mind.

Twelve

Wickfield decided to bring the day to a close with their delayed consideration of the development of the case. He and Spooner exchanged notes on their interviews of that afternoon, left the station, made their way to their usual public house, armed with pen and paper, and made themselves comfortable in a discrete alcove. Usually at this point the inspector would have invited his sergeant to open the batting with a sketch of the facts and the possibilities, but on this occasion, feeling overburdened with the weight of his reflections, he decided to divest himself first of his new suspicions.

'First of all, Sergeant, I must tell you of some further information I have been gathering this afternoon, after my interesting interview with Christopher Ross. I made a number of telephone calls. The first was to Damian Fay. I asked him how many people knew who his father was. "Few," he said, but he couldn't discount the possibility that his father had told more people than he knew of. He didn't think parishioners knew, but some of the clergy undoubtedly did, and of course his mother may have told people. I explained why we wished to know. I then phoned the housekeeper, Mrs Gould, and I asked her what she knew of Fr Wilfred's use of a sedative. She knew little. Her understanding was that he had obtained the drug quite legitimately on prescription having consulted his doctor, but she knew that his use was erratic, which the doctor could not have prescribed. She had once, a fortnight back, tackled him on the subject, and he replied that he took a capsule only when he felt the need; he didn't wish to form a habit by regular use, despite his physician's warning. While she was on the phone, I asked her whether she knew where Fr Gabriel had been the night of Fr Wilfred's murder. She said she didn't know but that, if he was true to form, he would have been round the parish visiting his flock. His day off was Wednesday. My third call was to the pathologist, whom I asked whether the wound that killed Fr Wilfred could have been self-inflicted. He had to consult his files – one could hardly expect him to keep in his head details of all the bodies he examines – and after a time he concurred that it could. "Unusual," he added, but possible.

'Now I come to the archbishop's call. Did I tell you he called? I did, good. Well, the unworthy thought occurred to me afterwards that perhaps he was fishing. His excuse for not telephoning us before was plausible but, I thought, insincere. In other words, he deliberately allowed the case to advance so far – my goodness, if only he knew! – before telephoning so that he could find out what we had uncovered.'

'I don't quite follow you, Sir. Why is that important?'

'Look, I'm going to speculate quite wildly, and take absolutely no notice, or rather tell me point blank, if you think I've taken leave of my senses. What if it had come to the archbishop's ears that Fr Wilfred had been guilty of another indiscretion: I don't know, he's abused youngsters, fathered another child, engaged in gun-running for the IRA, murdered a lover, robbed a bank. I leave you to imagine other possibilities, unlikely but still thinkable from what we know of the man. The archbishop takes exception to this act of folly, realises the harm it could to the Church's image if it got out and determines to stifle it at birth. He arranges for an assassin to remove the errant priest before he spills the beans or does whatever it is again or is found out. His call this evening was just to reassure himself that we hadn't yet uncovered anything untoward. He specifically asked me to hush up anything we *did* find out.'

Spooner looked flabbergasted.

'But, Sir, you don't know the first thing about the archbishop! He's possibly in line for multiple awards for saintliness, if there are such things.'

'I know, I know,' Wickfield said, 'but it is only an idea. If not the archbishop himself, perhaps the vicar general or the rural dean: how do I know? You must agree that we need to explore every conceivable avenue.'

'We do, Sir, but that particular avenue is a real bombshell.'

'Well, we shall leave it for the moment, but all the same I should like us to bear it in mind for a future occasion. If this case were a bit less confusing, we shouldn't need to be inventing improbable hypotheses! So, Sergeant, over to you.'

'Right, Sir, we seem to have three main options or possibilities: Fr Wilfred was murdered by a Roman Catholic; he was murdered by a rabid Protestant; or he committed suicide while under the influence of drugs. Shall I run through each one in turn?'

'Yes, do. I'm all ears.'

'First, then, he was murdered by one of his own kind. Here our way bifurcates.'

'It does what?'

'It bifurcates, Sir. It branches into two, depending on motive. On the one hand, we have a murderer who regards Fr Wilfred as a fossil holding up the march of the Catholic faith in difficult times; on the other, a murderer who regards the priest as a source of scandal who must be eliminated from the body ecclesiastic, like unworthy popes. Before we consider the drawbacks of that theory, who are our main suspects? Well, for the first option, we have Tabitha Warren, but also just possibly Thomas Foynes and Kylie Bradford; for the second, Christopher Ross, possibly Tabitha Warren, and possibly also, in the light of present thinking, the archbishop or his underlings.' He uttered this last phrase with more than a hint of irony. 'Secondly, however, we have to consider whether Fr Wilfred was killed by an enemy of the Catholic faith. We have not been able to identify any person or group in particular, but, as Fr Bancks warned us, the Election Covenanters, if we were going to choose, seem the most likely bunch. Our Mr Eton seemed the most aggressive, his alibi wasn't very solid, and we haven't met any of his flock. And one last possibility is that Fr Tarbuck committed suicide and that one of his flock covered up for him. The most likely candidate as the cover-upper is our old friend Mr Foynes, who seems to be cropping up a lot in our investigation. Now let's just weigh up the pros and cons of each hypothesis.'

'Crikey, Sergeant, whoever committed this murder, if murder it is, did a good job of concealing his tracks. How can it be so difficult to arrive at the truth?' Ignoring this little interjection, Spooner ploughed ahead.

'Hypothesis No.1: a parishioner did Fr Tarbuck in because he stood in the way of progress. This could be done through the grille that had been tampered with, but that really limits it to Miss Warren, as it seems improbable in the extreme that Mr Foynes reached across the priest's body to stab him, even if he could magic his way through the grille; or it could be done by someone – anyone – standing in front of the confessional. No such person was seen, but we now know there was a distraction on the other side of the church. If the distraction was accidental, the murderer took advantage of a unique opportunity and just happened to have a knife handy. Hm.

'Hypothesis No.2: a parishioner murdered Fr Tarbuck because he was a sinner and unfit to lead his parish. The question here is, how many people knew of Damian Fay? Otherwise Fr Tarbuck seems to have led a blameless and worthy life going back to 1918. If someone knew all along, why wait until now to strike? If, on the other hand, someone had only just found out, how did he or she do so, and why did it have such a devastating effect on their behaviour? In any case, whoever knows of Fr Tarbuck's liaison must also know, surely, that he wasn't in holy orders at the time. Your telephone-call of last night has revealed that at least some people were in the know.

'Hypothesis No.3: an enemy of the Church did away with the priest. The murder would have had to be done by someone standing in front of the priest as he sat in the confessional, since it is inconceivable that they risked being seen tampering with the grille or thought to be going to confession. We have no witnesses who remember a complete stranger in the church, and the same reservations apply as in No.2 above. Also, he would probably need to be left-handed.

'Hypothesis No.4: Fr Tarbuck took his own life, weighed down by the prospect of premature senility and the ending of his priesthood and confused by a sedative. This is possible – just – but then only Thomas Foynes can tell us, as only he could have removed the weapon.

'I suppose one should add in also Hypothesis No.5, as a subentry to No.1 above: the archbishop of Birmingham or a minion removed Fr Tarbuck to prevent the disclosure of some scandalous act. There are two main arguments against this theory – with respect, Sir: one, no stranger was seen in the church; two, we know of no such indiscretion, although we have asked the priest's sister, his curate, his superiors and quite a number of his prominent parishioners.'

'So, Sergeant, where in your opinion does that leave us?'

'It leaves us with an embarrassment of riches and no real evidence on which to arrest anyone.'

'If you had to choose? If the DCI makes it quite plain he wants an arrest and that he wants it now?'

'Well, Sir, I suppose it would have to be Miss Warren, the penultimate penitent in the line that evening but the last to use the altar-end, but I'd be very reluctant to believe it of her. On the other hand, I could believe Foynes made off with the knife, but it was a brave decision on the spur of the moment. I wonder whether he could be persuaded to confess to us. If it was Miss Warren, however, she and Foynes were in cahoots.'

'Right, we'll have another word with Miss W and Mr F, both of us, at the station first thing tomorrow morning. I'll leave it to you to arrange it.'

On that decisive point, their conference ended.

The following morning, however, a message awaited Inspector Wickfield. A Miss Warren had phoned the previous evening, wondering whether the inspector could oblige her with a moment of his time. Since she was suffering from a chill, could she possibly ask the inspector to call at her house: she felt unable to undertake the journey to Worcester. She had some information that might be useful to the police inquiry. Wickfield speculated and sighed. He decided to take Spooner with him, thus postponing, at least for an hour or two, their planned interview with Thomas Foynes. It was indeed an inclement day, with a wild wind blowing gusts of rain along the streets and lowering clouds sitting heavily on the city. The two men parked in Oakland Avenue, almost in front of Miss Warren's house, and this time, having shaken their macs and left them in the hall, they decided to accept their hostess's offer of tea. When all were settled, Miss Warren again thanked the men for making the journey and added that she hoped they would think it worth their while.

'You know,' she said, 'there's a little anecdote of d'Azeglio's that I thought matched this morning's little meeting. Did I tell you I was reading his memoirs? I did? Well, I'm now well into the second volume; most interesting, I can assure you, if a little bit higgledy-piggledy. Now he recalls an anecdote related to him by a member of the imperial household; he does not specify the date. This woman was what he calls a *dama di palazzo* – I take that to mean a sort of superior lady-in-waiting - to Marie-Louise of Austria – not that Austria's got any bearing on the story - Napoleon's wife, and they were holidaying at Saint-Cloud, not far from Versailles. Do stop me, Gentlemen, if you've heard this anecdote before.' They had not heard it before, which they indicated with grave and resigned shakes of the head. 'One day the party went out for a jaunt by carriage. It was wet and cold, and this particular lady-in-waiting was not feeling too good. The coach in which she was travelling was a covered landau, and word went out from the emperor that all the coaches were to uncover. But why would you say that? Anyway, having no intention of sitting in the open air, she argued with the equerry, made pretence of negotiating, argued again, and finally she got her way. She commented to d'Azeglio – much later in life, this was - that she had defeated Napoleon before Wellington did! Now isn't that a splendid little story? Stand up to authority, and they crumple! Typical of the cowards.'

'Now, Miss Warren,' Wickfield said after a small cough, anxious to stem the tide of anecdote, in case there were more on the way, 'you said you had something to tell us.'

'I did, and now the moment of revelation has arrived, I do feel slightly nervous about it. Just take no notice of me for a moment while I collect my thoughts.' She fussed around with her cup and saucer, and swept a hand over her bedraggled white hair, and shifted position in her chair.

'Inspector, Sergeant. What I am about to tell you is not exactly secret, otherwise I shouldn't be telling you, but as far as I know, only one other person in the world, apart from myself, is aware of it – of the full story, that is. I confess I have not been quite honest with you. That is, I have told you absolutely nothing that is not the truth, but I have withheld from you a piece of information that might, just might, be relevant to your present inquiries.' Here she paused and seemed to hesitate as to whether to continue at all.

'Yes, please go on, Miss Warren. We shall treat anything you tell us with the utmost discretion. You say it might or might not be relevant. Well, if it's irrelevant, it will go no further than these four walls. If it's relevant, you will have given us material help.'

'Well, I rather skated over my uncle Brian's clerical career when I last saw you, didn't I? What I could have, and perhaps should have,

131

told you at the time was that in 1934 he filled in for a few months as parish priest *extraordinaire*, as you might say, at St Patrick's in Walsall: it was the old church then, of course. I forget whether the priest in charge was off sick, or on compassionate leave, or away for some other reason, but my uncle was airlifted in as an emergency measure. The neighbouring parish clergy covered for *him* in his absence from his own parish. It turned out he was in that parish for nearly nine months. Now the curate already in the parish, but only by a month or so, had been ordained eight or nine years and so was considered rather a novice in the job: the Church moves quite slowly, you know! But that's all by the way. His name was Wilfred Tarbuck: an earnest young man, apparently, well thought of by his superiors, keen to learn, and agreeable to the ladies of the parish. My uncle and he knitted well together. There was quite an age difference, almost inevitably in any parish priest-curate relationship, but it didn't seem to matter. You understand that I'm telling you all this from my uncle's point of view. Warren is a common enough name, and as far as I know, Fr Wilfred never made the connection between his temporary parish priest in Walsall in 1934 and elderly Miss Warren, his parishioner in Droitwich, in 1946. He certainly never mentioned the matter to me, and I never mentioned it to him.

'One evening, so my uncle told me, there was a visitor at the presbytery door asking for Fr Tarbuck. He thought the youth rather uncouth, clearly not flush with money, rather aggressive in his speech and angry to be told that the curate was out visiting. There being nothing Uncle Brian could do about any of this, he merely wondered politely whether the man would be able to call back the following morning, when Fr Tarbuck was almost sure to be in. He was abused for his pains, but the visitor left without causing any further trouble. Because he was new to the parish, my uncle took no particular notice, thinking that it was quite normal for the young man to be acquainted with the curate but not with the acting parish priest.

'Some months passed, and the young man appeared again. Almost the same scene took place: nobody's "fault", just one of those things. The man went away again, but this time my uncle remembered to tell his curate about the visitor. Fr Tarbuck was visibly moved, he said; concerned, but worried rather than frightened. It was then that his curate confided in Uncle Brian, and the story he told ran something like this. When Fr Wilfred took a

132

year out, between junior seminary and senior seminary, he worked as a filing-clerk for a firm in Smethwick. There he met a young woman his own age, called Ann Fay, and it seems that relations were cordial to the point of carnal knowledge. You will understand, Gentlemen, that I am not sitting in judgment: I am merely relating to you what my uncle told me. In due course she gave birth to a son. Now it so happened that at the same time, or perhaps a little later, Ann's unmarried sister, who was only a year or two older, also gave birth to a son, and she expected the same treatment for her baby. The family declined to help out. Their reason was this. Ann was a serious girl who had got herself in a bit of a mess but made the best of it. Dot, that's the sister, was a promiscuous hussy – those were my uncle's words, presumably repeating them from Fr Wilfred's account – and had to lie on the bed she had made – so to speak. Dot therefore put her child up for adoption, effectively washing her hands of him. Now the thing is this. She claimed that Fr Wilfred – plain Wilf Tarbuck as he was then, all of eighteen years old and a clerk with few prospects – was the father of her child, a thing he strenuously denied. Ann backed him up, and so did Ann's parents, but of course there would always be a doubt in their minds when Dot was so adamant and vociferous about it. The trouble was, there was more than a passing physical likeness between the baby and the alleged father. Perhaps you would wish to object that it's impossible to tell at that age. No other man stepped forward to claim the child as his own, so there were two consequences: the child was given up for adoption, as I say, and a doubt hovered in the minds of Ann's family, which they could never quite put behind them.

'Some years later, Dot's son's adoptive family – their name was Perkins – let slip who his real parents were: or perhaps I should say alleged parents. This was in the course of a family row, in which the Perkinses revealed to the sixteen-year-old boy that he was not their real son, that he was nothing but trouble, that they would be glad to see the back of him, and that if he darkened their door no more, they would not shed a single tear. This was tantamount to throwing the boy out, and out he duly went, to seek his way in the world as best he could. Anyway, the young John Perkins' first point of call, or perhaps his second, was his supposed biological father, and he called at St Patrick's presbytery before Father Wilfred had been temporarily appointed there. Fr Wilfred spoke to him, treated him kindly, gave him a few quid to see him on his way, but firmly refused to take any responsibility for him. He said he must return to the Fays in Smethwick and ask them about his true paternity: his mother Dorothy would probably know (or possibly not!). He himself knew nothing about it, was certainly not himself involved, and felt that he could not, as a curate with little money to spare, undertake the further education or apprenticeship or whatever was required of a youth whom he had met for the first time that day and of whom he knew nothing.

'When John Perkins called on the second and third occasions, when my uncle met him on the doorstep, Fr Wilfred then spoke to his parish priest to ask for his advice. Did he have any responsibility for his young lover's sister's illegitimate child? My uncle, who was a balanced and pious sort of man, if a little eccentric theologically speaking, was quite firm that he did not – if, of course, his side of the story was true, which he did not doubt. There was endless scope here for scandal if Fr Wilfred acknowledged any sort of connection with a wild youth claiming him as his father. Any hand-out or leg-up would be misconstrued by malicious folk, who would do anything to twist events to the Church's detriment.

'My uncle then left the parish to return to his own, and he rarely saw Fr Tarbuck after that, and never for any length of time. However, they did meet once more, in a more leisurely fashion. It came about in this way. More tea, Gentlemen?'

They both accepted another cup from the seemingly bottomless china pot, complete with rose-red tea-cosy. Miss Warren shuffled out into the kitchen for some more biscuits.

'When my uncle was eighty,' she resumed, 'he decided, in consultation with the archbishop, to call it a day, and he retired to the old priests' home at Sedgley. Another resident there was Fr Wall, who had been Fr Tarbuck's parish priest at Aston. Word went out that Fr Wall had not long to go, and Fr Tarbuck went over to visit him for one last time. This was in 1948 or 49, I should think, not long after Fr Tarbuck had been appointed here. When he had had his last conversation with Fr Wall, he spied my uncle in a corner and went over to say hello. My uncle, who had not, I'm glad to say, retired into a self-absorbed nostalgia, as so many old people do, eagerly inquired after Wilfred's health and career in the intervening fifteen years since their time together in Walsall. Father Wilfred decided to confide in him. The two went out into the garden, and chose a shady spot under a wych-elm where they could talk undisturbed. The sun was warm, birds were busy in the shrubs, bees bumbled about, as bees do, and all in all it was a scene calculated to inspire unhurried confidences.

'It transpired that John Perkins had reappeared from time to time, as expected, I suppose, and Fr Tarbuck had always given him a few quid but no more and had always made it plain that his modest alms were out of charity, not justice. The boy had been called up in 1940 and had not been seen around Birmingham for some time. When he was demobbed in 1945, finding himself at a loose end and with no particular ties, he had gone off to some South American country as a mercenary. There he had been seriously injured and had had more or less to crawl back to the United Kingdom nursing his wounds and the last of his funds. It was just before Fr Tarbuck visited my uncle that John Perkins broke into the Sacred Heart presbytery at dead of night, threatened Fr Wilfred with a knife and succeeded in escaping with the Sunday's takings. He would have been about thirty at this time. Fr Wilfred had no hesitation and no compunction in reporting the culprit to the police, and at his trial Perkins swore that he would get his own back for what he saw as treachery. So, Gentlemen, that's a very long-winded way of telling you that Fr Wilfred had a mortal enemy out there who may or may not be responsible for his death.'

The old lady sat back in her chair at the end of this narrative, as if to rest.

'There are several questions that spring to mind, Miss Warren,' said Wickfield. 'First of all, why did your uncle tell you all this, and secondly, why have you only just decided to tell us?'

'Let me take your second question first, Inspector. I read in this week's paper that three men had succeeded in escaping from Armley gaol near Leeds, and that the public were on no account to approach them. They were named as Bert Wyllie, Sam "The Snake" Corder – and John Perkins. It may not be the same John Perkins, of course, but it alerted me to the old story. The answer to your first question is this. As my uncle neared his end, I used to visit him regularly at Sedgley. On one of these occasions he told me what he knew about Perkins, with two important comments. Firstly, he said he did not regard Fr Wilfred's confidences as coming under the seal of the confessional: Fr Wilfred had spoken as man to man, not as confessed to confessor. Secondly, he believed that Fr Wilfred was in danger, and he told me that, if anything happened to him, I was to inform the police if I thought it appropriate. I have considered it now my duty to tell you all this, even though I may be maligning a completely innocent man. I make no accusations, you understand, but the implication of what my uncle told me is that Perkins is now a suspect, however remote.'

'May I ask you a question, Miss Warren?' said Spooner.

'Of course, Sergeant. Fire away.'

'Have you any reason to believe that John Perkins has put in an appearance at Droitwich since the events of 1948?'

'No, none. There has not been a whisper, as far as I am aware, of mysterious strangers or threats, veiled or otherwise, or anything similar. My impression from the newspaper article, however, is that Perkins has spent much more time inside than out in the last fifteen years, so maybe he hasn't had a chance to show up. He'd be what? about fifty by now: high time he was settling down.'

Temporarily suspending further questioning, Wickfield and Spooner thanked Miss Warren cordially for her hospitality and for her information and returned to Worcester to join in a manhunt for an escaped convict.

Thirteen

*T*he most pressing task was to contact the Yorkshire police to find out the extent to which they had succeeded in tracing John Perkins, on the run from Armley prison. Wickfield spoke to a Superintendent Richard Joyce.

'Well, the men escaped three weeks ago. We caught two of them pretty quickly: only Perkins is left. Now our experience of Perkins is that he's a slippery customer. He uses aliases, he dodges about, he has a number of criminal friends who put him for a few days at a time, and so on. In a few weeks, say six or seven, he'll have managed to grow a beard or a moustache which will alter his appearance. He'll have a change of hair-style, and he'll try to melt into the background. As always, his trouble is going to be to get a job. He escaped once before, but we caught him when he turned to his old craft of burglary. A bloke's got to live.'

'Is his mother still alive?'

'Yes, she is, still in Smethwick. The local lads are keeping a watch on her house, but I think Perkins is probably too wily to try to make contact just yet a while.'

'What about his father?'

'He's always said he never knew who his father was.'

'Siblings?'

'None that we know of.'

'I'm just playing with the idea that he was in Droitwich on 8 February, which would be five or six days after his escape. Are you aware of any friends of his in the area?'

'No, he could be anywhere. He'll make a mistake, and then we'll have him.'

'What's he in for?'

'Aggravated robbery.'

'Is he dangerous?'

'We're telling the public he is, and I think that's probably true, but only if cornered.'

'So you're not actively looking for him?'

'We are and we aren't. There's nobody out there detailed to trace his movements – very difficult that, if not impossible – but his details have been circulated to all the forces, and we hope that folks will keep their eyes peeled.'

Wickfield consulted the circular. Below the picture of a middle-aged man, with puffy cheeks, rather narrow eyes, a small mouth and a thoroughly seedy expression was the following information:

Wanted, escaped from Armley Prison on 6 February 2009, John Ronald Perkins, aged 50, medium height and build, brown hair, green eyes, heavy jowls, one gold tooth. Should not be approached by the public. Is likely to head for the Midlands.

Wickfield wondered, not for the first time, at the infinite variety of the human physiognomy. Given that the number of features was strictly limited: a forehead, two eyes, a nose, two cheeks, two ears, a mouth and a chin, that no two human beings were so close as to be indistinguishable, with the rarest exceptions, was an astonishing feat of nature. Conversely, where there were no obvious distinguishing marks, virtually any description one cared to fashion could apply equally to individuals that were numbered in their thousands, if not their millions. It was all rather discouraging.

However, the end of his search was not so long in the coming as he had feared. He received a telephone-call that evening from Fr Griffin, the acting parish priest at the Sacred Heart, with a piece of information and a request.

'You see, Inspector,' he said, 'we've not yet spoken to the people of the parish in any but the most desultory terms. We haven't exactly ignored Fr Wilfred's murder, but we haven't yet hit on the way we

138

could properly talk about it from the pulpit; and in any case, I wasn't here that first Sunday. So two Sundays have now gone by, and nothing's been said apart from platitudes. This coming Sunday, Gabriel and I have agreed that we must devote the best part of the sermon to the subject, and he is going to speak at all the Masses! This seems proper, as I never met Fr Wilfred, and the people will take it better coming from Gabriel than from me. We are convinced that one of the parishioners is responsible: we just don't see who else it could be. We are also pretty clear that it had to be one of those who went to confession, probably one of the last two, but of course, we cannot conceivably make such accusations from the pulpit, which is dedicated to the Word of God! So we thought that Gabriel should couch his words in terms of a general appeal to conscience, hoping to strike home where the evil is. However, he would like you or your sergeant to be there, so that if any member of the congregation should be moved to public contrition, the police would be on hand to bring the matter to an immediate, formal and business-like conclusion. Would that be possible, do you think?'

'What exactly is Fr Gabriel going to say?'

'Ah, well, you'll have to ask him that yourself. When we discussed the matter at lunch, I know that he hadn't got any but the very vaguest thoughts on the subject. Perhaps we should wait and see? The Spirit will inspire him, I'm sure.'

Wickfield and Spooner divided the four Sunday Masses up between them – neither of them very enthusiastic, it has to be admitted – and it fell to Wickfield's lot to attend the eleven o'clock service. This was the most popular of the four, and the church was nearly full – and that meant a full quota of undisciplined children. The Mass was said by Fr Hugh, but at the appointed time Fr Gabriel put in his appearance, formally robed in black cassock, white cotta and purple stole, acknowledged the celebrant with a stately bow and slowly mounted the steps into the pulpit. He looked quietly graver than Wickfield had so far seen him, and somehow suffused with a sense of purpose and serenity that he had not looked for in a man who could run away when matters troubled him. He could have been only twenty-six or twenty-seven years old, and yet at that moment Wickfield would not have hesitated to entrust the management of his soul to this young and fervent pastor. Although the inspector was unaware of it at the time, Fr Gabriel had sought the archbishop's permission to change the middle reading for a short passage from St Paul's second letter to the Corinthians, so that he could preach on the text, '*Now is the favourable time; this is the day of salvation*' in chapter 6. (Before the happy publication of the *Jerusalem Bible* in 1966, Fr Gabriel would have been preaching on the Douai text: 'Now is the acceptable time; behold, now is the day of salvation'. He thought that the 'Behold' would have grated on his listeners' sensibilities!)

Instead of launching into his homily, however, Fr Gabriel slowly withdrew a coin from the pocket of his cassock and began to tap the base of the microphone with deliberation. 'Tick, tock,' he said. Wickfield realised afterwards that this, simple as it was, was the master-stroke which rendered the sermon both effective and utterly memorable. 'Tick, tock.' The tapping and the slow accompanying words continued for a short while. 'Tick, tock, tick, tock.' The tapping continued, as it were in the background, as the preacher broached his theme. 'I want you to imagine,' he said, 'the apostle Paul in Corinth, the red-light district of the Mediterranean, struggling to implant the Christian message in the early years of the 50s of the first century. Here was a man eaten up with the love of God, consumed with an unquenchable fire, and in the unlikely setting of Corinth, over eighteen months during which he plied his trade as a tent-maker, he established the Christian gospel, founding a number of small groups based in people's homes. He then moved on to Ephesus, across the Aegean Sea, where he spent the next two and a half years.'

The tick-tock continued quietly, as all eyes in the church were fixed hypnotically on the young preacher in the pulpit.

'Unfortunately, bad news reached Paul in his Ephesian roost. Troublemakers had arrived in Corinth after his departure and were undoing his good work. They were deriding Paul's authority to speak in the Church's name; they dismissed him as insignificant in appearance, a poor speaker and a charlatan. Now these people were Christians, with letters of commendation from other churches! They were working against Paul for their own aggrandisement, claiming apostolic authority, the right to be supported by the congregation, the honours due to officials of the Christian body. Paul, as you can understand, was outraged. Here not only were eighteen months' work being destroyed before his very eyes, as it were, but more importantly, the gospel to which he had devoted the last twenty years of his life was being twisted out of true, distorted in the name of earthly values. It was a mockery. His first measure was to pen a firm letter of rebuke. What could have possessed the Corinthians to abandon the Gospel of truth so easily? These men were nothing but mountebanks!'

The tick-tocking continued without interruption, a gentle reminder to the congregation, no less plain for being unspoken, that time was ineluctably passing.

'Now the letter we know as Two Corinthians is probably an assembly of five shorter letters, or fragments of letters, roughly cobbled together, and it takes a little ingenuity to tease them apart. This isn't me talking, you understand, My Friends: I'm simply giving you the conclusions of scholars in the field! The part we've read from today belongs to the first of the letters. The news of the disturbance in Corinth has just reached Paul. His reputation has been attacked, the Corinthians are wavering in their allegiance, it's touch and go whether they abandon Paul's understanding of the Gospel in favour of some other coarse and worldly interpretation. I can see him now, in his Greek villa in Ephesus. Incidentally, if you go to Ephesus today and tread the very streets that Paul trod, you will wonder that the city is five miles from the sea, whereas in Paul's time it was a busy port! The river has silted up, My Friends; nature never stands still. Anyhow, there is Paul in his modest villa, pacing up and down in his agony of thought, while dictating to a scribe; or perhaps, of course, he was writing the letter himself, feverishly scribbling on the papyrus with a clumsy quill. His thoughts come rushing in, he can hardly contain himself. The truth is being distorted! Great heavens, what can he say to stop the rot? Holy Spirit, come to my aid!

'He says two things. First of all, his authority is not manifested in spectacular miracles, stunning revelations from on high, a lavish life-style in supposed keeping with his position as an apostle. No, unequivocally not. His authority can be seen in his weakness as a speaker, in his sufferings for the sake of the Gospel, in his modest work as a tent-maker in his own financial support. *These* are the things that mark him out as an apostle of the Lord, as one who relies on God to bring his work to fruition. My Friends, when I pass on to the Great Pulpit in the sky and stand face to face with God, the one person I shall ask to meet first is Paul! What a man! What a hero! What a model for any and every Christian! But I digress. Secondly, in this first letter of reproach to the Corinthians, he warns them that time is running out. Between Jesus' death and his return in majesty, God has granted a short space of time for repentance. Those caught so to speak with their trousers down when the moment of judgment arrives have, according to St Paul, had it! How is it that the Corinthians think they have all the time in the world to flirt with impostors and their frivolous novelties? He, Paul, had personally handed the Gospel over to them. They are utterly foolish even to consider exchanging it for a fake. They must repent at once, or they may be taken unawares: and then what?'

Here the preacher paused, but the steady ticking continued, a permanent and mesmerising accompaniment to this most vivid and heartfelt of all sermons.

'Now Fr Wilfred was murdered in this church a matter of sixteen days ago: a harmless, devoted and holy priest going about his sacramental business in the Lord's name. Somebody somewhere knows who did it and why. I am appealing to that person to come forward, here, today. Death is uncertain. I would not wish that person to be caught unawares without the time to make his or her peace with God. We are fortunate to have with us in the congregation today one of the detectives responsible for the inquiry into Fr Wilfred's death. I beg the wrongdoer to make him or herself known after church, by some hint or sign or message, and all will be well. As Paul tells us in today's text, "Now is the favourable time; this is the day of salvation".'

The preacher stopped abruptly. More dramatically, the ticking stopped. The profoundest possible silence fell on the church. Wickfield could not remember a more dramatic and electrifying moment in all his years of church-going. It was masterly, unbeatable, supreme, a moment to savour for the rest of his life, and he knew then that Fr Gabriel had the makings of a tremendous preacher; but would his appeal work?

It was as Wickfield was delighting in the theatrical wizardry and theological expertise, not to mention the rhetorical skill, which had produced this moment, that a man leaped to his feet in the middle of the church and shouted out, 'I didn't do it, it was nothing to do with me!' All eyes swivelled round to focus on this stranger in their midst, a man of average height and build, with brown hair and green eyes and heavy jowls. 'I didn't do it,' he repeated. 'I know you've been getting at me, you're trying to make me confess.' He waved a finger at the priest in the pulpit, as he shouted his words of self-exculpation down the church. 'But I won't confess to something I never did. Why should I kill my own father?' The sensation in the congregation was palpable. Never again would they witness such real-life drama, not if they lived to be a hundred. Several men, probably seated so that they could take up the collection a little further into the service, made as if to lay hands on the man and forcibly remove him from the church. Fr Gabriel intervened.

'No, no, no violence, please. I appeal for calm. This man is entitled to speak in front of us if he wishes, provided that he observes due moderation. Now, My Friend, do you wish to say anything more?' The man, however, said nothing more but made his way hurriedly past the people in his pew, down the aisle and so out of the church, to be speedily followed, inevitably, by Detective Inspector Wickfield of Worcestershire CID.

Wickfield caught up with his quarry as the latter was striding down the Worcester Road seemingly intent on putting as much distance between himself and the church as possible. With a little persuasion Perkins agreed to accompany the inspector back to Worcester station in the latter's car. At the very least, Perkins would have to be returned to prison to face the penalties for escaping. Once ensconced in one of the station cells, the prisoner calmed down sufficiently to tell the inspector his story.

'I had nothing to do with Fr Wilfred's death,' he said. 'I heard about it only yesterday, when I arrived from Birmingham. I was sitting in a pub last night and overheard a couple of blokes talking about it – how slow the police were, and why didn't they get a move on, and I'd soon show 'em, and it must be that last geezer who went to confession.'

It dawned on Wickfield at that moment that perhaps he was doing Thomas Foynes an injustice: either he should arrest the man on suspicion of murder, or he should take steps to clear him publicly of all implication. However, he focussed again on his prisoner.

'I strolled over and asked for more information. I got a long story – how true it was, I've no means of telling, but I presume the gist of it was OK. Was I shocked? I'd never got close to Dad, because he wouldn't let me; refused to acknowledge me; said my birth was nothing to do with him. Mum always went on about the priest being my father, so what was I to believe? Wilfred was kind. Gave me small amounts of money every so often. Perhaps he wasn't my father, except that Mum said he was. Sometimes I hated him; then I found I needed him. No one else ever came forward to say, Yes, this is my son and I'm proud of him. I didn't really know who I was. I yearned for a father. Why couldn't Wilfred have just said I was his son, even though it wasn't true? It would have made such a difference to me. Instead, I've turned out rotten, a real no-good'un.'

'Where were you on the evening of 8 February? I've got to ask, you see.'

'Look, I didn't do it. I was way up in Yorkshire.'

'Can you prove it?'

'Yes, I certainly can. I'm not telling you how I've managed since I escaped, but I can tell you this much without getting anybody into trouble: for the first three nights, I hid out with a mate of mine, never mind where, then I took a room for two nights, then I moved on again to another mate's. Now I was in that room on 7 and 8 February, so I couldn't have done a murder down in Worcester, could I? You've only got to ask the landlord.'

'OK, we can check that out. Tell me, have you any idea who might wish to kill Fr Tarbuck?'

Perkins shook his head. 'None,' he said.

When Wickfield was satisfied that he had gathered as much relevant information as he could from John Perkins, he returned to Droitwich for his turn of duty at the 6.30 Mass, but nothing untoward transpired. Fr Gabriel was just as fresh and inspired on his fourth delivery of the sermon as on his third, and it occurred to Wickfield that he, Wickfield, might one Sunday return to the Sacred Heart, Droitwich, with his wife, just for the pleasure of hearing the young man expatiate from the pulpit. In the meantime he had arranged to meet Spooner back at the station later that evening to compare notes on the day's events. Spooner had nothing to report, but he did make this comment:

'My word, Sir, that young man can speak! The congregation were mesmerised. I shouldn't mind going to church more often if all sermons were like that!'

Wickfield related in turn his encounter with John Perkins and added a piece of home-spun psychology.

'What that man is suffering from is a delayed, or perhaps prolonged would be a better word, Oedipus complex, you mark my words. He never grew out of the Oedipal phase in his teens, or for that matter first time round in his childhood. He learnt to hate his father as a rival for his mother's affections, and by that I mean that the conundrum of his father's identity took over any sort of affection he could feel for his substitute mother, and yet in his saner moments he latched on to his father – or alleged father – as the key to his own identity. That's if our friend Dr Freud is right, of course. The poor man has been put through the wringer owing to his mother's refusal to disclose who his real father was. My guess is that she hit on Wilfred Tarbuck as an easy and believable option, because her own life was so chaotic she didn't have a clue who Perkins' father was, and yet she wouldn't acknowledge that to her family, for fear of appearing promiscuous. Disgusting!'

'So has the little experiment produced no useful results?'

'No, it doesn't seem to have done.' In that, however, he was not quite accurate.

Two days later, two letters arrived for the inspector at the station. Both were anonymous. Their contents gave Wickfield much food for thought. The first was in a non-descript buff envelope franked in Droitwich. The handwriting was as if a right-handed person were using his or her left hand (Wickfield thought).

Dear Inspector Wickfield (it ran)

You may be surprised to hear from me, but I wanted to set your mind at rest, if that is possible in view of my natural wish to remain anonymous. I saw you at church on Sunday, and I guess that you were as moved by Fr Gabriel's sermon as I was. I have confessed to my crime. I couldn't let Fr Wilfred continue, and I realised at a certain point that I was the only one willing to stop him. I am not going to commit any other murders: there is absolutely no cause to do so. So you may safely drop your investigation in the knowledge that the one responsible for Fr Wilfred's death has made his peace with God. Please return to Worcester with a light heart and explain to your superior that the case is solved.

Kind regards

A Friend of Priestly Loyalty

What on earth was that about? Wickfield struggled to make sense of it, and yet somehow there was a ring of truth. He felt he should follow it up with Fr Griffin.

The second letter, in a white envelope size 6¾ and consisting of laboriously pasted words from a newspaper, had been posted in Birmingham.

To Whom It May Concern

Look no further for your murderer: I AM. The Whore of Babylon has been dealt a bloody blow. The Dragon has left the sea to devour the Whore's Offspring. More will follow.

This was a deal more sinister. Was it a death-threat? Were Fr Griffin and Fr Winterton in danger?

Armed with photocopies, Wickfield and Spooner drove up to Droitwich to consult the local clergy. Fr Gabriel was out at Oscott, on one of the monthly 'training' sessions organised for recently ordained clergy, but Fr Hugh was happy to receive them. Wickfield had no hesitation in showing the priest the two letters. After some minutes the priest looked up from his perusal of the two notes, scrutinised the addresses and the postmarks and then looked as baffled as the detectives. He was short and wiry, with deep-set, intelligent eyes and a large chin. Wickfield put his age at about forty.

'Let us just suppose for one moment that the first one is genuine,' Wickfield said. 'The writer certainly gives the impression of being a parishioner of yours, of having attended Mass on Sunday, and of

146

knowing about confession. If this person confessed to you, would you tell us?'

'Oh, no, you know I couldn't do that.'

'Can you tell me whether anyone has confessed? There's no need to tell me who it is, if you know or guessed.'

'You know I can't, Inspector. Nothing that takes place in the confessional can be revealed.'

'Let's just say someone has confessed to you to the murder of Fr Wilfred. What would you do?'

'I could do two things. I could urge the penitent to go to the police. This would be particularly important if an innocent person was in danger of being suspected of the crime, but I don't think that's the case here – is it, Inspector?' he asked dryly. 'No offence intended! And I could refuse to give him absolution if I considered his going to the police essential, to give evidence of his good faith and to prove his contrition.'

'So what did you do?'

'Oh, no, Inspector, that's unworthy of you! My lips are sealed, as you well know.'

'Could this person have confessed to Fr Gabriel?'

'I can tell you that: no. At his request, and with the archbishop's acquiescence, Fr Gabriel has not been hearing confessions in the parish since the murder. He wishes most earnestly to avoid precisely the sort of situation you envisage. He will return to the confessional when you have caught the murderer. Perhaps I should say, *if* you catch the murderer. Sorry, Inspector, that's only me being mischievous again. Take no notice! On the other hand, your letter-writer doesn't say he went to confession here in Droitwich: it could have been to any priest anywhere; and in any case he – or she – doesn't specify that the confession was to a priest: it could have been in the secrecy of the heart, to God.'

'Would another priest elsewhere have taken the same line as you and urged the person to give himself up?'

'Yes, that would be the norm. Let me just explain, Inspector, to make the matter perfectly clear. You may have heard of the *Code of Canon Law*, which contains nearly 2500 regulations that govern the management of the Catholic Church. Some forty of them concern the practice of confession, and all priests have to be familiar with them.

One of them, for example, says that the seal of the confession is *inviolabile*: inviolable, with no exceptions. But on top of the *Code of Canon Law* there is a detailed Holy Office *Instruction* dating from 1915, and especially a three-volume work on confession, or at least the sacraments in general, by a Spaniard – at least, I think he was a Spaniard – called Noldin, which covers confession from every angle, exhaustively. This is the standard textbook in seminaries. Of course, seminarians can't master all this material, but the main principles are drummed in so that major mistakes are avoided. Let me give you an example I remember from my seminary days. Suppose a girl comes to confession wishing to be forgiven for a sin against chastity committed with her boyfriend. She is contrite, and you give her absolution. The following day her boyfriend comes to confession. "My girl-friend was in yesterday and said she found your comments helpful." He proceeds to confess his sins, but he makes no mention of the sin of unchastity. Do you gently remind him, or do you say nothing and let him leave you with a grave sin on his conscience? Here's another example, of which I was reminded when I came to this parish and saw our grand confessional – the one, unfortunately, in which Fr Wilfred met his death. You move the slide across at the conclusion to one penitent's confession and begin to hear the confession of the person who has been waiting at the other side. "I heard what that other person said, Father," your penitent begins, "and I feel I must tell someone about it." What do you say? There are also some sins that cannot be forgiven by a priest: the person who admits to them must be told to go to the local bishop, the matter is so serious. There is even one sin that only the pope himself can forgive! And so on. There are endless problems and difficulties that lie in wait for the unwary confessor, but my brief reply to your question, Inspector, is that, while some confessional practice is left to the priest's discretion and experience, the main principles are laid down and form the common structure for all priests.'

'OK, Fr Hugh, thank you for that. What do you think the writer means by "A Friend of Priestly Loyalty"?'

'I'm not sure. It's a curious phrase, isn't it? Priests are loyal to their calling or their bishop or their Church, and in a number of ways: by being celibate, or holy, or pastoral, or obedient, or respectful, or dedicated. Heaven knows what the writer had in mind. The phrase suggests that Fr Wilfred was killed because he wasn't in some way "loyal", or am I reading too much into it?'

'No, I get that out of it, too, but as to what the writer is thinking of, your guess is as good as mine. What do you make of the other letter?'

'Well, the "I AM" is rather curious. As you know, it's sometimes used as a title for God, but here you'd expect the writer to say, "I am he". What the writer wanted to say was, "I am she", but that would give the game away, so she opted for something less gender-ridden.'

'Wouldn't you expect, "Look no further for your murderer: it's me"?

'Yes, perhaps. And the "To Whom It May Concern" strikes me as odd, as if the writer didn't know your name. Doesn't that suggest someone not in the parish? After all, your name's been in the papers enough!'

'Yes, maybe,' Wickfield sighed. 'And the Birmingham postmark: if the writer lives in Birmingham, what is he or she doing murdering clergy in Droitwich? It's all such a puzzle. Right, we'll take up no more of your time, Father, but go away and think things over. Pray for our enlightenment!'

Fourteen

'**W**e're not making progress, Sergeant. We're stuck, jammed, wedged; we're surrounded by conflicting data, surmise, suspicion and an ocean of possibilities, and do you know whom I blame? You! You're paid to think, and you haven't come up with a single viable hypothesis for – well, for ages.'

'What about you, Sir?'

'Me? I must wait for the inspiration of my muse.' He uttered these portentous words with his eyes closed and his face raised to the ceiling. 'My ideas don't come to order, you know: they're much more sophisticated than that.'

'And who is your particular muse, Sir, if I may ask? Not Urania, the muse of star-gazers, by any chance?'

'No, not Urania, Sergeant. Do you know, I despise your sense of humour. It's Melpomene, the muse of tragedy, and sometimes Thalia, the muse of comedy, but I admit that neither is speaking to me at the moment. In fact, neither has spoken to me for a fortnight. What a disaster! The DCI will pull us off the case and consign us to outer darkness as a pair of incompetents. I shall end up with early retirement, doomed to cultivate vegetables when I'm just entering my prime, while you – '

'With all respect, Sir, only you will have to take the rap. I shall be promoted to inspector as a reward for having survived six months as your deputy.'

'Yes, very funny, Sergeant.' He paused uncertainly. 'OK, to business. There are a number of things we need to do to enable us to focus. Firstly, two things need to be done to prevent immediate injustice. We have to instruct Fr Hugh to give it out from the pulpit that there is no truth in the rumour that Fr Wilfred, of saintly memory, fathered John Perkins: that's a piece of scandal we must sit on, even if it's true! And we have to clear Thomas Foynes' name, at least until we can provide incontrovertible proof to the contrary: innuendo and rumour will damage him if we don't make a move. At the same time, Miss Warren's possible role, in a conspiracy with Foynes, will have to be re-examined. Secondly, if these last two steps enable us to eliminate murder through the grille of the confessional, we can concentrate on a murderer leaning into the priest's compartment. That person could be parishioner or stranger, but either way, somebody must have seen something. I'm not about to believe in praeternatural agency, diabolic intervention, voodoo or black magic as an instrument of Fr Wilfred's death.'

'Thank you, Sir, credit at last! That was my idea, and I produced it only ten days ago!'

'Very well, Sergeant, if scoring petty points and quibbling over details make you happy.' He sniffed pointedly but with the utmost good-humour. 'It did seem unlikely, mainly because no one in the church recognised such a person, but having eliminated everything else, we are forced to fall back on it again as our only option. The breaking of the vase camouflaged the murderer's action admirably. To proceed. A further re-enactment might meet the case, this time including the broken vase, but people's memories are doubtless fading. If our first letter is genuine, we're looking for a parishioner, and probably, or at least possibly, someone who knew of Fr Wilfred's teenage indiscretion. Two questions need to be thought about: why did the murderer strike only now? and why is an indiscretion *before* priestly training considered so dire as to merit death? One person in our drama I think we have not considered closely enough is Damian Fay. We know he was in the church, we know he was seen, we know he did not go away after seeing Fr Wilfred, except to regain his car, and we have only his word for it that he walked out of the church at half-past six. What if he returned to the church later on during that session of confessions, and no one took any notice because his face or form were familiar? Isn't there a Sherlock Holmes story in which no one sees the milkman because he is not *remarkable*?

'Thirdly, we need to eliminate suicide. I regard suicide as an improbable occurrence, but it is not laughable, and we need to exclude it if we are to go forward. Again, our friend Mr Foynes is the only possible witness. This is what I propose, therefore. We need to re-interview Damian Fay, Thomas Foynes, Miss Warren and the other members of that original small congregation. We also need to go back over all the testimonies that we have gathered, from the archbishop down, because somewhere in all that information may be lurking the one detail that gives us the clue to the puzzle. I can't help feeling that we have come face to face with the murderer but have failed to recognise him – or her, of course. He's laughing at us as we stumble around. I tell you what: if we haven't identified him by the end of this week, I shall hand in my resignation. How's that? I feel that frustrated.'

They caught up with Thomas Foynes as he was beginning his lunch-break, and they thought it best to drive to the station so that the interview could take place in formal surroundings and be recorded. After the conventional legal preliminaries, Wickfield impressed on Mr Foynes his need to make a truthful statement in a murder inquiry.

'We should like to eliminate you from our investigation,' he said, 'but we cannot do so until you have had one further opportunity to give us your account of the events surrounding the death of Fr Tarbuck on Thursday 8 February. Your three previous statements have been apparently candid and full, but two suspicions remain. Let me be perfectly frank with you, Mr Foynes. We should like to believe you to be completely innocent, but you must satisfy us on two points. On one hypothesis that implicates you, which we haven't mentioned to you before, Miss Warren committed the murder when Fr Wilfred was hearing her confession, and when you went to confession a few minutes later, the priest was consequently already dead, but you pretended to us and to everybody else that he was still alive. Your only purpose in this manoeuvre was to protect Miss Warren. The two of you were therefore in the scheme together. Would you care to comment?'

'Inspector, that's a fantastic notion! Miss Warren commit murder? I admit I don't know the woman very well, but that just seems too preposterous altogether. Well, whether she committed murder or not, I can tell you with absolute honesty that Fr Wilfred heard my confession and that he was still alive when I left the box. What more can I say?'

'Very well, let us come to our second hypothesis, Mr Foynes, of which you denied all knowledge previously. You now have another opportunity to come clean, that is to say, to tell us the truth. It has occurred to us that Fr Wilfred committed suicide, while the balance of his mind was disturbed, let us say, and that you got wind of his intentions while you were in the confessional. You ran round to his part of the confessional, seized the knife and hid it on your person, so that when Mr Jennings came to wake him up for Benediction, it looked like murder.'

'And what would be my intention, Inspector?' Foynes did not seem in the slightest discomposed by the interrogation.

'You admired Fr Wilfred and wished to save him from the indignity of suicide in the church.'

'Yes, it's a neat idea, but it happens to be quite untrue. Let me say this, Inspector. There are something like nine suicides in the Bible – it's difficult to say in every case whether a death, for example Samson's, should be classed as suicide – but in none is the reaction judgment and condemnation. The people who wrote the Bible are satisfied with recording the facts, or what were thought to be the facts, and then to leave judgment to God. If Fr Wilfred committed suicide, it would be best to let the facts speak for themselves and for us to feel sorrow at a human life cut short but not to cast blame. I should not have dreamed of interfering in the course of events.'

'But you might have thought that *other people* would condemn Fr Wilfred for his final act of defiance, and you wished to preserve him from such unfair judgment.'

'No, Inspector, I should be in favour of enlightening people about what the Bible says and does not say, not in perpetuating mistaken notions of divine disapproval. In its *Declaration on Religious Freedom*, Vatican II specifically lays a duty on all to assist one another in the quest for truth.'

'We shall ask you to read and sign a typed statement in due course, Mr Foynes. Thank you for your cooperation.'

In deference to her age and less than perfect health, Wickfield agreed with Spooner that Miss Warren could be interviewed in her home, with the precaution that a WPC should accompany them to tape-record the interview and to add gravity to the proceedings.

153

'I wonder whether we shall be given another dollop of d'Azeglio,' Spooner asked on their way to Droitwich.

'Well, if it puts the old lady at her ease, why not? She could be throwing buckets of boiling oil over us from her bedroom windows.'

Miss Warren was effusively welcoming and insisted on cups of tea all round.

'I was just about to take my usual forty winks,' she explained, 'and I never do so without a cup of tea to settle the stomach. You will just have to join me! Sergeant, would you mind doing the honours? Four mugs in the cupboard above the cooker, sugar on the side, milk in the fridge, and tea beside the kettle. Teaspoons are in the drawer by the sink. I know you'll be interested to hear that I'm just coming to the end of the second volume of d'Azeglio's memoirs - unfortunately. I think I told you I was reading them, didn't I? Well, he tells the sad, or possibly happy, story of a young girl stood up on her wedding day. I should perhaps explain that the author, then in his twenties, was staying in the hills outside Rome learning his craft as an artist, and he got to know a prominent local family – only peasant, you know, but influential. He describes the daughter of the house in terms that appalled me: the colour of boiled potatoes, he says, with faded eyes like bubbles of oil in pap and the most apathetic creature in the world. Anyway, on the day of the wedding, the only thing missing was the groom, and he failed to put in an appearance at all. Curiously, the bride was apparently quite unmoved by it all and went on later to marry another young man from Rome whom d'Azeglio describes as *un mezzo signorotto da dozzina*: such a wonderful phrase, Inspector: half a man, and he was only an ordinary one to start with! Goodness me.

'However, in the next chapter is a comment that I thought could apply to the Sacred Heart, Droitwich in 1968! I'm not boring you, am I? Just stop me if I am, but while we're waiting for our mug of tea, I might just as well tell you this. D'Azeglio was talking to a friar from Piedmont, who told him that the Piedmontese are lovely people but, once inflamed with drink, resort to profanities and knives at the drop of a hat. D'Azeglio comments that he had found exactly the same with the people of the Roman countryside amongst whom he was living. Once their blood is up, he says, they bring out the knives and then, he adds, they dodge into the nearest church or chapel where they are safe from the long arm of the law. It does seem that our murderer has made himself safe by committing his crime in a church!'

Seeing the look on Wickfield's face, she hastily appended a disclaimer.

'I'm being mischievous, of course, Inspector and Constable. Just my quirky sense of humour.'

Further conversation was interrupted by the arrival of Sergeant Spooner with a tea-tray, and then Wickfield made a start on the formal interview.

'Miss Warren, this is a formal interview –' indicating the police woman – 'because we are not yet confident that you have told us the whole truth. You have consistently said that the murder of Fr Wilfred was the work of an outsider, attributable variously, if my memory serves me correctly, to a fifth-columnist, "someone out there who is on the rampage", an infiltrator and a purported son of Fr Wilfred. You have also more than once drawn our attention to a novel by the still happily living Miss Heyer. Now these suggestions could be attempts on your part to distract us from the truth.'

'What is that supposed to mean, Inspector?' Miss Warren asked with outrage, pretended or real, in her voice.

'It means that you yourself are under suspicion of Fr Wilfred's murder.'

'Me, Inspector? But that's preposterous. How would I have done it, for a start? And why should I? Why, I liked the man, for all his faults. Have you taken leave of your senses?' She appealed to all three members of the police-force.

'We cannot expect you to admit knowledge of it, Miss Warren, but I can tell you that the grille in the altar-end of the confessional had been tampered with so that it could be removed and replaced easily, in seconds. Now you went to confession in that end of the confessional. If you, or possibly an accomplice, were responsible for the tampering, you could have removed the grille, stabbed Fr Wilfred, replaced the grille and left the box as if nothing had happened. Very neat. I congratulate you.'

'You're mad, Inspector, if I may say so. Someone went to confession after me. Wouldn't they have noticed the priest was dead? This is all absolute nonsense. I must appeal to your commonsense, Inspector: do I honestly look like a murderess to you?'

'The thought that occurred to us, Miss Warren, is that Mr Foynes, who succeeded you in the confessional, agreed with you beforehand to *pretend* to go to confession, so that all suspicion would be deflected from you. In other words, the two of you were in it together, to do away with Fr Wilfred.'

'But I hardly know Mr Foynes! The idea of agreeing with him to murder Fr Wilfred is simply nonsensical. It doesn't even begin to stand up.'

'Did you know that the grille had been the subject of interference?'

'No, not the faintest idea: it would never have occurred to me. This is all so fantastic, Inspector, I can hardly believe the evidence of my own ears.'

No amount of questioning would persuade Miss Warren to alter her story, and Wickfield had to admit that her denials seemed perfectly genuine. Eventually the investigating team left Miss Warren to her siesta.

That evening, nursing a metaphorical headache brought on by the complexity and yet apparent simplicity of the case, Wickfield decided to go over all his notes again, in the hope that light would dawn. After a supper of kippers and chips and bread-and-butter pudding, Wickfield and his wife Beth retired to the cosy disorder of their sitting-room to pursue their respective diversions. They had drawn the curtains against the chill and darkness of the late February night, and an easy stillness reigned. That is to say, Wickfield shuffled his papers, Beth turned the pages of her book, but otherwise all was quiet. At a certain point, Beth closed her book with a sigh and said, 'Yes, a good book, that: I enjoyed it.'

Only too anxious to have an excuse to abandon his rebellious notes, her husband inquired what book it was to which she referred.

'Nicholas Montserrat's *Something to Hide*,' she replied.

'I think I read that last year, or perhaps the year before. Remind me of the story.'

'A lorry-driver called Carter gives a lift to a distressed-looking girl thumbing a lift at the roadside, and that simple act of kindness leads to a nightmare.'

'Yes, well, go on.'

'She turns out to be pregnant. Partly out of sympathy, and then in response to her threats, he lets her stay in his house until the birth. She then does a bunk, leaving him with a dead baby on his hands. He decides to burn the body in his boiler, but a neighbour recognises the smell of burning flesh and calls the police.'

'Yes, go on, it's coming back.'

'Well, the upshot is that under persistent questioning, Carter confesses to having buried his wife in his garden years before. "Something to hide", you see. It's not a full-length novel: more of a novella, but I've enjoyed it.'

Wickfield sat on, saying nothing, ruminating. His features were immobile. He did not stir in his chair, until, after the passage of a considerable amount of time, he folded his notes away and took out a crossword, still in silence. Eventually he said,

'This moment deserves a little something, my dear. Shall we have a drop of port?'

Beth looked at him for an explanation.

'Earlier today, I threatened to resign if I hadn't solved this case by Saturday. I now shan't have to, as I've solved it, four days early!' He looked very pleased with himself. 'It's a bit late to telephone Fr Gabriel, but I shall do so first thing in the morning. Boy, am I looking forward to this!'

However, in the morning, he was destined to be disappointed. Fr Hugh answered the telephone.

'It was really Fr Gabriel to whom I wished to speak,' he said apologetically. 'Is he available?'

'No, I'm afraid not, Inspector. Can I help?'

'Can you tell me when I can get hold of him?'

Wickfield detected a hesitation at the other end of the line.

'Well, to be honest with you, Inspector, he's having a spot of leave – with the archbishop's permission. I'm not sure when he'll be back.'

This was a bit of blow, but not catastrophic.

'Yesterday you told me he was attending some course at Oscott. Isn't his absence somewhat sudden?'

'I was guilty of a little bit of a lie, I'm afraid, Inspector. He asked for Monday as his day off, and then he phoned through to say that he was having a little time off, and he had squared it with the arch. That's all I can tell you, really.'

Wickfield came off the telephone thoughtful. He put through a call to the archbishop.

'Fr Winterton? Just having a little bit of a break, Inspector. He'll be back in due course, I daresay.'

'You know we're involved in a murder investigation here. I need to speak to Fr Gabriel.'

'Well, I appreciate your concern, but the welfare of our priests takes precedence over an investigation which can possibly wait a week or two.'

After a second's thought, Wickfield persisted.

'Your Grace, would you do me a favour? Would you contact Fr Gabriel with a message from me? Would you tell him that I know who the murderer is and that I now need Gabriel's help in a little drama? He is not in the slightest danger, but I need him to preach at the Masses on Sunday. Will you pass this message on, please? It's very important. I want him to ring me at the earliest opportunity.'

'Very well, Inspector, but I cannot guarantee what his reaction will be, and I shall certainly not put any pressure on him to comply.'

Fifteen

Sunday 3 March, the first Sunday of Lent, dawned bright and cold.

The wind had fallen, the clouds had dispersed, but the sun, not long risen, shed no warmth. The worshippers arrived at the Sacred Heart for the eight o'clock Mass, well-wrapped. Some who skipped their weekly obligation during the year made an effort to attend in Lent, acknowledging the importance of this time of preparation for Easter. While not by any means full, as the clergy expected for the later Masses of the morning, the church was busy enough, with people settling into their seats, saying their rosary, lighting candles, reading their daily missals, exchanging whispered greetings or absorbed in prayer. Wickfield was glad that it was the earliest Mass of the day: fewer people to upset, less possibility of a slip-up.

The Mass began. Fr Gabriel, in his purple – some might call them violet – vestments, intoned the by now familiar vernacular greeting addressed to the people, and the response followed in confused unison. Mass had begun. The priest looked young and somehow innocent, fresh and homely, and yet there could be no doubting either his competence or his seriousness. The first reading, on which he intended to base his sermon, was from the nineteenth chapter of the Old Testament prophet Jeremiah and would happily give him scope for his histrionic proclivities. (I withdraw that phrase: it should have read, 'for his dramatic abilities humbly harnessed in the service of Scripture'.)

Then the Lord said to Jeremiah, 'Go and buy an earthenware jug. Take some of the elders of the people and some priests with you. Go out towards the Valley of Ben-hinnom, as far as the entry of the Gate of the Potsherds. There proclaim the words I shall speak to you. You are to say:

"Kings of Judah, citizens of Jerusalem! Listen to the word of the Lord! The Lord of Hosts, the God of Israel, says this: I am bringing down such a disaster on this place that the ears of everyone who hears of it will ring. This is because they have abandoned me, have profaned this place, have offered incense here to alien gods which neither they, nor their ancestors, nor the kings of Judah, ever knew before. They have filled this place with the blood of the innocent. So now the days are coming – it is the Lord who speaks – when people will call this place no longer Topheth but Valley of Slaughter. I will make this city a desolation, a derision; every passer-by will be appalled at it and whistle in amazement at such calamity."

You are to break this jug in front of the men who are with you and say to them, 'The Lord of Hosts says this: I am going to break this people and this city just as one breaks a potter's jar, irreparably'.

The psalm, the second reading, the gospel all followed without drama, and as the latter ended, Fr Gabriel moved from the lectern and its attendant microphone to the centre of the sanctuary steps, from where he could address the congregation without barrier or intermediary, person to person, preacher to listener, teacher to recipient: as it were intimately, familiarly. From under the lectern he had taken a porcelain milk-jug, procured by the housekeeper for a few pence at a bric-à-brac stall in the town the previous day: spout and handle intact, a small chip on the lip, white with a bunch of myosotis on the side. This he held in his hands, passing it from one to the other, thus quietly capturing the congregation's attention. After a few moments' pause heavy with expectation, he began.

'Let us return in our minds, My Friends, to the year 600 BC. We are citizens of Jerusalem, a handsome and bustling city of the Middle East, the proud possessor of a history going back at least five hundred years. We are Jews, supposedly dedicated to the God of Israel, but in fact many of us now worship the Canaanite god Baal. We have abandoned the strict moral code of the Law of Moses, laid down half a millennium previously, and now self-seeking and slaughter are the order of the day. We go about our business, but we are fearful because thefts and muggings, instead of the warm, gracious peace that God promised us, stalk the city. Violence reigns. We hurry to return to our homes, but even there we shall not be safe. What a situation! We cannot blame only our leaders: over the years, we have all been involved, by committing acts of aggression ourselves, or by not protesting at wrong-doing, or by ignoring the demands of justice. Will the Lord not rescue us from our own folly and weakness?

'Yes, the Lord has heard our cry for help.' Fr Gabriel flourished the jug. Bearing the end of the reading in mind, some of the congregation must have wondered what would ensue. 'There is one man in the city he has called up, singled out from before his birth to be a channel of justice and peace and true morality. His name is Jeremiah, which means Raised by the Lord. There are nine other Jeremiahs in the Bible, but this is the famous one, justly so. He is the son of a priest in the city. At the time of these events, he is, I suppose, in his mid-forties, a lonely, shy man, constantly begging God to leave him alone and find someone else for his dirty work, constantly, like Jonah, trying to escape from God's imperious will. He is the butt of insults and ill-treatment, there are plots against his life, he is dismissed as a fraud and an impostor. Few give him even the time of day. In the opposite corner, as we might say, is the king, Jehoiakim, not on any account to be confused with his successor Jehoiachin! Jehoiakim is a puppet of the elders and princes, intent on feathering his own nest and those of his cronies and content to let the wider country degenerate into chaos. At this time, our poor country, so sadly reduced since the glorious days of king David, is threatened by two powerful neighbours vying for supremacy in the Middle East: on the one hand Assyria, which is roughly what we call Iraq today, and on the other Egypt, and we are likely to be squashed in the middle. Ignoring Jeremiah's advice, which is based on God's wishes for his people, Jehoaikim goes his own way, dithers, takes poor advice, and it is only a matter of time before his political vacillation takes its disastrous toll. My Friends, we are heading for a calamity! Time and again God pleads with us through this humble priest's son to return to him, but the prophet's voice is derided and ignored. Nothing Jeremiah says or does can stem the decline, so obstinate are we and our leaders, and in twenty-three years from now, to Jeremiah's immense grief and misery, Jerusalem is reduced to rubble, its temple destroyed and we are carried off to Babylon as slaves. It is to be very nearly the end of the Jewish race. In the ensuing chaos, Jeremiah, humble, despised, obedient Jeremiah, is carried off as a slave to Egypt, and there, tradition has it, he ends his days, unmourned and forgotten. Well, not quite forgotten, but you know what I mean.'

All this time, Fr Gabriel stood there calmly, clearly himself part of the scene he was conjuring up for his listeners. He kept passing the jug slowly from hand to hand.

'As we hurry towards home with our shopping,' he continued, ' – although, heaven knows, the shops stock little enough these days - we see Jeremiah addressing a group of elders and priests and beckoning them to follow him to the south of the small, crowded city. We follow, out of curiosity. The little party, gathering extras on the way, make for the gate variously called the Dung Gate or Gate of the Potsherds. Jeremiah's patched robes wave round his legs, his worn sandals slap on the stones that form the surface of the street. His whole appearance is unprepossessing. At the gate Jeremiah stops and turns round, indicating the view in front of him. We all stand and look back past the old quarter, the City of David, to the temple on its extended hill beyond. From under his robes, Jeremiah produces a potter's jug and flourishes it over his head with an outstretched arm. "Do you see this jug?" he shouts. "This is you! Listen to a message from your God!" We, his audience, are spellbound, stunned into silence by his authority. We gaze open-mouthed at this simple man grasped, despite himself, by God's spirit of rhetorical power. "You are scum! You have abandoned the ways of your fathers. You have lusted after foreign gods. You have filled this place with innocent blood. And in particular you, who should be leaders and teachers, have betrayed your calling by peddling lies and murdering holy men.'

Here, dramatically, Fr Gabriel indicated the confessional a third of the way down the church to his left.

'And do you know what God, my God and yours, intends to do with you? Shall I tell you? He will smash you as a man might smash a potter's jar!'

With these words, Fr Gabriel hurled his jug across the church, where it shattered against the wall by the confessional. The congregation were stunned. Not a sound was heard, as Fr Gabriel stood stock still at the climax to his sermon. There was a silence as deep as the grave.

The silence was broken by a strangled cry from beside the altar. 'You've betrayed me! I unburdened myself to you, to ease my conscience, to seek the Lord's forgiveness, and you have shouted out my guilt in public. What sort of priest are you?' Here Basil Jennings, tearing at his cotta, rushed from the sanctuary into the sacristy, whence proceeded sounds of a scuffle, the banging of a door and then silence. The congregation, uncertain what to do next, sat in astonished immobility. Slowly Detective Inspector Wickfield rose from his pew near the front of the church, mounted the chancel step and addressed the church from near where Fr Gabriel stood.

'Ladies and Gentlemen,' he said, 'I must apologise for this little drama. May I explain? My name is Wickfield, and I have been in charge of the hunt for Fr Wilfred's murderer. I have realised for some days who the killer was, but I could not find any proof. My idea was therefore to engage Fr Gabriel to enact a little scene in the hopes that the emotion of the moment would persuade our killer to reveal himself. It worked. I wish to add, however, that Fr Gabriel is absolutely and completely innocent of betraying any confidences made in confession. I have no idea whether Mr Jennings confessed to Fr Gabriel; perhaps he did, perhaps he didn't. It doesn't matter. Fr Gabriel used words in his sermon that I dictated to him, basing myself on our inquiry and on a hunch. At no time did I ask him to comment or to commit himself. Am I right, Father?' He turned to the priest, who nodded his acquiescence. 'We shall never know for certain, despite what Mr Jennings might protest, whether he ever confessed his crime to a priest or not, and be assured that no priest will ever reveal that information. Ladies and Gentlemen, we have our killer. One final word. Some of you may have heard that last week a gentleman was moved to speak at the 11 o'clock Mass, claiming to be Fr Wilfred's son. I can assure you that we have not the slightest reason to believe him to be telling the truth: it is a slur on the character of a worthy and holy priest, so you can forget all about it. Now please, I invite you to carry on with your act of worship as if nothing had happened.'

As he stepped off the chancel and made his way towards the back of the church, he heard Fr Gabriel asking the people to stand for the creed, and as he left the building, he heard the voices of the people raised in unison in their profession of faith.

That afternoon, Wickfield explained the case to his sergeant as they sat at a lakeside café near the city, imbibing tea and munching scones. Parents had brought their little ones out, despite the cold wind, to feed the waterfowl or stroll round the lake; fathers knocked a ball around with their sons; courting couples mooched through the trees, hand in hand. No one took any notice of the two men in a corner of the café discussing the murder of Fr Wilfred Tarbuck.

'It was that Tuesday evening,' Wickfield said, 'as I sat over my mountain of notes, bereft of ideas, or rather drowning in a welter of ideas: Beth reminded me of a Montserrat story in which a man hides a guilty secret for years, only to have it forced out of him by an unlikely event. I had a vision of the man in the story standing in front of his boiler feeding in the body of the girl's dead baby. He'd given this girl a lift, you see, and her thanks were to land him with an infant corpse before running off. That immediately gave me the germ of an idea for the murderer's motive and identity. I realised how blind I'd been. We'd perceived the difficulties in supposing that the murder was committed through a grille – not the physical difficulties but the improbability of the suspects – and alternatively in arguing to suicide. We, or at least I, ended up giving most weight to the idea of someone standing in front of the middle of the confessional box, even though the other people in the church couldn't recall anything unusual. You yourself pointed out a very large snag in not coupling such an act with the destruction of the vase, if the breakage was purely accidental, and yet Mrs Ryan did not come through as an accomplice to murder. It dawned on me suddenly, with a staggering sense of my own inanity, that the one person who had stood in front of Fr Wilfred and had been seen by everyone must be the murderer. We had taken at face value everyone's assessment of what he had been doing there: he had – hadn't he? – been waking the priest up. But what if his motives had been more sinister? It did not take a Beerbohm Tree to part the curtain, lean in with a left hand clutching a short knife, stab the priest while pretending to shake him by the shoulder and withdraw as the victim tumbled out, without arousing suspicion. In the fracas, Jennings quietly slipped the knife into his pocket, nonchalantly joining the parishioners in the presbytery with the body.

'As I sat in my armchair absorbing these rays of illumination, I pondered Jennings' motive as reflected in Montserrat's story. He did not figure in any of the most active parish groups we considered. As he was a server and quasi-sacristan, he did not seem to nurse a personal hatred of his parish priest. I then realised that his motive was not hatred but fear. The "unlikely event" which triggered that fear was Fr Wilfred's visit to the psycho-geriatrician in the wake of the increasing unreliability of his memory. It came to seem probable to me that Jennings had in the past confessed to some misdeed which now he was frightened Fr Wilfred would reveal, either in a moment of absent-mindedness or through forgetting where he had heard it. For example, let us say Jennings had murdered his wife, as in *Something to Hide*. Fr Wilfred might have woken up one morning, saying to himself as he shaved, Hey, I forgot to tell the police that I saw Jennings murder his wife, or, Great heavens, I was meant to pass on to the police some information about the death of Jennings' wife. Jennings was not prepared to risk this.

'Now he knew that Fr Wilfred had been given phenobarbital by his doctor but that he took it erratically. On the night of his death, the priest had taken a capsule in the sacristy prior to hearing confessions. This is in line with what we know of Fr Wilfred's own state of mind: he feared for his role as a confessor and was doubtful about how long he could keep with it, in view of the danger of breaking its seal. He therefore became particularly anxious at confession time. Knowing that the priest became drowsy after taking one of his capsules, Jennings had a good half-hour to prepare his little strategy, psychologically – in his determination to go ahead – and materially – by getting a knife, so that, in the likely event of having to wake the confessor up before Benediction, Jennings was ready. That evening, or the following day, he doctored one of the grilles in the confessional, to distract attention from his own role in the priest's death. If anyone had seen him in the church at an unusual hour or in an unusual place, he could always manufacture some excuse: he had mislaid some beads from his rosary, or someone had complained about a protruding nail: not difficult to a man used to hearing the pupils' excuses for not having handed in homework.'

'And did he send us the *Bloodletting* booklet for the same reason?' Spooner asked.

'He did: anything to keep us from thinking about his presence in the church and his proximity to the priest that evening. I've asked myself where he could have laid his hands on a copy. We know from the author's niece, our avid reader of nineteenth-century Italian memoirs by a certain Piedmontese nobleman, that there were not many copies in existence but that the ones that did exist had been given away, for the most part, to the author's fellow-priests. It was easy for me to imagine the sequence of events. Basil gets to hear of this booklet either through Fr David directly or through the group to which Mr Christopher Ross belonged and which had been aided by Fr David. We know that Miss Warren also made no secret of owning a copy. Jennings then reasons that, as these priestly recipients die off, their effects are cleared out and sold off, as none of them, by definition(!), has family. The priests' effects are likely to be dealt with by Birmingham enterprises. Somewhere in the city, therefore, is a second-hand bookshop which has on its shelves a copy of *Bloodletting in the Body Ecclesiastic*, just waiting for a discerning purchaser to pick it up. He comes to hear, or already knows, that Oscott has a copy but would only *loan* it and in any case requires a name and an address. It is safer, and more interesting, to spend a few days rummaging around Birmingham's old bookshops, and we know he found one in less than ten days. To make sure we focussed on the idea of decapitating a Church group, he cut out the first two sections, leaving us only with a dubious account of murdered popes. In any case, the booklet was not crucial to his strategy.

'Now we thought that our little drama with the tick-tocking microphone last Sunday produced little result: an Oedipal complexive shouting about his relationship to the late Fr Wilfred and two cranky letters. My bet is that the longer of the two letters was genuine. If you read it again in the light of who the murderer was, you can see that it makes a certain rough sense. He realised that he was the only person willing to *kill* to preserve the confidentiality of the confessional. His own secret being safe once Fr Wilfred was dealt with, there was no need for him to contemplate further murders of priests. However, one result we had not catered for was that Jennings was moved by Fr Gabriel's sermon to go to confession, to ease his mind. Now the confession sessions scheduled for that week were the coming Thursday and then yesterday morning, but Jennings couldn't wait that long. He therefore approached Fr Gabriel privately, probably on that Sunday afternoon. We know that Fr Gabriel wasn't hearing confessions in the parish for a while, but when Jennings comes up to him and asks for a quiet word, his guard would be down: Jennings could wish to speak to him on a variety of topics. He would not, and probably in Church law could not legally, refuse the man confession. Whether he gave him absolution, as Jennings' letter implies, I'm not so sure. This unexpected and unwelcome revelation tips the priest's equanimity over the edge, and he again does a bunk, hiding I know not where, but this time with some sort of explanation to the archbishop and with the latter's agreement. I was encouraged in this reading of the facts by the use of a particular word by the archbishop. He said over the telephone that "the *welfare* of our priests takes precedence over the police investigation", not, "the *safety* of our priests takes precedence etc". In the archbishop's mind, therefore, Fr Gabriel was not in any *physical* danger – as possibly intimated by our second anonymous letter – but needed some time to recover his mental or emotional health.

'Anyway, Fr Gabriel then, in his place of concealment – Oscott would be a very agreeable spot for a few weeks' seclusion!– gets my message. Because I tell him I know who the murderer is, he is not in any danger of breaking the seal of the confessional. When I approach him with my idea for a particular sermon for today, I do not ask him whether Jennings has been to him to confession; I do not allude to the possibility at all, even obliquely. All he has to do is to go along with my charade. I must add that the sermon was entirely of his own construction: a brilliant piece of theatre. All I asked him to include was a reference to a teacher peddling untruths and to the shedding of innocent blood in the house of God. Those two clauses would, I hoped, work on the sacristan's conscience sufficiently for him to betray himself. The rest Fr Gabriel engineered, and his Old Testament scene was probably more influential in bringing about the dénouement we witnessed than my own little contribution.

'I explained to Fr Gabriel how I had drawn my conclusions about the murder, so that, if Jennings had confessed to him, there would be no need for him to admit it or make disclaimers; I wished him to know categorically that I was not sounding him for information – for *any* kind of information. I asked him at what Mass Jennings would be acting as server today. I arranged for two uniform to slip into the sacristy from the presbytery after the start of Mass, and for two to wait outside the church at the back: those were the only two exits from which Jennings could effect his escape if he decided to make a run for it. I myself sat at the front of the congregation, in the event, which I considered unlikely, that Jennings in his desperation and chagrin made a lunge at the priest. That just about wraps it up, I think.'

'What if Jennings hadn't made a move at the end of the sermon?'

'Ah, there we should have been stuck, I fear, as we should have no proof of his guilt. All the eye-witnesses of the killing would agree that Jennings was called on by those present to act as waker-upper, that he hesitated, and that he merely shook the priest by the shoulder: that is what they saw, because that is what they expected to see. I noticed from this morning's Mass that Jennings is left-handed. If he thought of disguising this fact by stabbing the priest in his left-hand side, he probably dismissed the thought with the realisation that he could botch the job by using his right – in this case wrong - hand. He tampered with the grille at the altar-end of the confessional to highlight the wound in the priest's *right* side. By now, he would have got rid of the knife in any one of a thousand ways, and of any of his clothes which showed blood-stains from the blade as he secreted it beneath the folds of his cotta or cassock. We should have nothing with which to go before a jury. No, all in all, Fr Gabriel's oratorical skills won the day.

'You know, Balzac has a very interesting comment, which could apply to our entire investigation in the murky corners of Worcestershire. One of his characters says, "*Si l'on s'est tant battu pour la religion, il faut donc que Dieu en ait bien imparfaitement bâti l'édifice*": if people have fought so much for religion, it must be because God constructed the building with too many faults!* Our interviews have highlighted such rifts and divisions that even I, cynic that I am, had not imagined, and that's in one religion only!

'May I leave you with one final thought, Sergeant: if I ever mumble again about my muses deserting me, you can remind me that my muse is – always - Beth!'

---

* Pierre-Joseph Genestas in *Le médecin de campagne*, chap.3 (or 4 or 20, depending on editions!). JF.